"Treasure is often found in the act of discovery, rather than in the discovery of the treasure itself."

"I seek nothing. I possess everything I desire," DìNes managed to assert, albeit with a hint of doubt clouding his voice.

Caught in the ethereal conversation, DìNes found himself grappling with truths he had long chosen to ignore. The conversation spiraled, touching upon the depths of his desires, the void in his existence, and the facade of his complacent life. As quickly as it appeared, the illuminating star retreated, blending with the distant celestial bodies, leaving DìNes in contemplative darkness. Shaken, he returned to the bedroom, uncertainty clinging to him like a second skin. Amoremea remained unchanged, a silent witness to an encounter that left DìNes questioning the very foundation of his existence. Why was this happening why now? Life was…good from his perspective.

The Acquisition of VàsSon

A Story Based on the Pursuit of Maturation

By

Vonda Li

Acknowledgements

I begin with profound gratitude to my Creator. Although this book is not biblically based, the gifts and talents I've utilized in its creation are blessings from my Heavenly Father.

I owe a deep debt of gratitude to my mother, who not only passed on her creative spirit but also continually encouraged me to thrive, embrace challenges, and remain fearless.

To my sister Judy, whose inspiration has been a beacon for me, reminding me to seize every opportunity, I offer heartfelt thanks. Similarly, my sister Angie has been a pillar of support, never letting me waver or lose heart.

A poignant acknowledgment goes to those with whom I've parted ways as I ventured on this journey solo. Your absence paradoxically served as an inspiration. The experiences and lessons gleaned from our shared past were invaluable catalysts for this work.

To you, the reader, my sincere appreciation for choosing this book. An author pours heart and soul into their work, and my hope is that the passion and thought invested here resonates with you. Although the genre of this book is fiction, a distinct message weaves its way through the narrative. May this message captivate and inspire you just as the process of writing did for me.

About the Author

Vonda Li is no stranger to the world of writing. Though many of her previous works remained unpublished, she now bravely ventures into the literary market, buoyed by strong encouragement and hope. Vonda's aspiration is not merely for her books to be sold, but for them to resonate deeply within the hearts of her readers.

Specializing in fiction, her narratives are brimming with drama, adventure, and romance. Vonda crafts characters with such depth and richness that readers easily find a piece of themselves in each one. Her tales often extend beyond a single book, leading to captivating sequels or even full-blown series. Texas, her home, is the birthplace of all her stories and serves as a constant source of inspiration.

Table of Contents

Chapter One

"The Confrontation"

Nestled at the tip of the coast of Île Sainte-Marguerite, amidst a lavish display of nature's grandeur, resided a complex figure known as DiNes VàsSon. A man largely ensconced within his own world, DiNes ventured out into the social sphere primarily to fulfill his desires, only to retreat back into his solitude once satiated. His captivating beauty was not lost on him; he flaunted it extravagantly, adorning himself in the finest garments that accentuated his allure. This innate talent for enhancing his beauty was not just a personal indulgence but a magnet that drew relentless attention wherever he roamed.

DiNes sauntered through the town with a feigned annoyance at the attention he attracted, a spectacle that did not go unnoticed by the locals. He was the embodiment of desire and envy, a figure admired fervently by both women and men. For many women, the mere thought of lying beside him or possessing a fragment of his beauty became a fervent desire. Men, too, found themselves captivated, either wishing to emulate his demeanor or yearning for his companionship.

To be seen in the illustrious company of DiNes VàsSon was akin to acquiring a coveted badge of high social standing. The mere whisper of one's association with him bestowed an instant elevation to elite status. Previously inaccessible doors swung open, revealing circles that thrived on social prestige and exclusivity. Everyone, it seemed, longed for a nod of acknowledgment from DiNes VàsSon or an invitation to the grandiose social gatherings graced by his presence.

Gossip swirled incessantly throughout the town, with everyone keen to know who had recently graced the illustrious company of DiNes VàsSon. Aware of the swirling rumors, DiNes addressed some, lending them either validity or dismissal with a casual grace. Others, he chose to ignore, weary of the relentless pursuit that marked him as a prized catch, an entity to be hunted and claimed. Increasingly, he felt surrounded by vultures and malevolent spirits, entities eager to extinguish the radiant light that emanated from within him. A creeping disillusionment began to shroud DiNes, as the joys and pleasures of life seemed to drift further away from his grasp. He had indulged in the finest dining, adorned himself in garments of unparalleled luxury, and shared intimate moments with the most glamorous women. His company had been sought by kings, vassals, and members of the high aristocracy, yet a void persisted, gnawing at his contentment.

Frequently, he found himself pondering, "What is next?" An undercurrent of frustration and impulsive dissatisfaction spurred him to abandon the island periodically, seeking fresh territories to conquer and possess. Yet, each venture proved futile, leading him back to his starting point within a year, discontentment in tow. Eventually, a despondent DiNes relinquished the dream of finding fulfillment elsewhere. Resigned, he sank into a routine that saw him associating with forbidden companions, succumbing to the allure of the darker corners of society...

One evening, DiNes jolted awake from a slumber induced by potent spirits, gasping for breath and clutching his throat, as if emerging from the grasp of a black smoky cloud that threatened to choke him in his dreams. Beside him, in a state resembling a coma, lay the beautiful Amoremea, a woman revered as the island's unparalleled beauty, a formidable figure much like DiNes himself. He gazed at her with wide, frantic eyes, a flicker of suspicion igniting in his mind. Could she have been the malevolent force strangling him in his sleep? Leaning over cautiously to confirm her unconscious state, a demanding whisper interrupted his thoughts. "DiNes," it resonated, pulling his attention towards the veranda. Panicked, DiNes sprung from the bed, hastily wrapping a sheet around his waist. "Who is here? What do you want with me?" he called out, his voice echoing through the silence. No response greeted him as he ventured towards the veranda, the whisper repeating, drawing him out into the moonlit night. Underneath the gaze of a full moon, accompanied by a sprinkling of stars, DiNes found himself alone on the veranda. Yet, one star seemed to defy the natural order, drawing nearer, its intense glow warming, almost scorching his skin.

"DiNes WHAT DO YOU WANT!!" The illusory celestial voice roared. This voice frighten DiNes leaving him perplexed and confused no longer was he bold and curious, he was timid and disturbed by the over whelming presence of this intrusive voice. Backing away, DiNes stumbled into a chair, his focus locked onto the advancing abyss. 'DiNes!' the voice now intensified and demanding a response. "Why are you hesitant, how long will you keep me waiting?" The voice commanded.

"I... what do you want from me?" he stammered, the enormity of the moment rendering him almost paralyzed. "I seek nothing. I possess everything I desire," DiNes managed to assert, albeit with a hint of doubt clouding his voice. "Are you certain, DiNes?" the celestial entity inquired, its voice resonating with an ageless wisdom. "Your soul seems restless, yearning for something undefined."

Caught in the ethereal conversation, DiNes found himself grappling with truths he had long chosen to ignore. The conversation spiraled, touching upon the depths of his desires, the void in his existence, and the facade of his complacent life. As quickly as it appeared, the illuminating star retreated, blending with the distant celestial bodies, leaving DiNes in contemplative darkness. Shaken, he returned to the bedroom, uncertainty clinging to him like a second skin. Amoremea remained unchanged, a silent witness to an encounter that left DiNes questioning the very foundation of his existence. Why was this happening why now. Life was...good from his perspective.

A week later, DiNes was once again enveloped in the suffocating grip of intoxication, collapsed like a discarded doll in his lavish chair. The ambiance in the room was disrupted as the now familiar voice pierced the fog of his drunkenness. His glance swept wildly around the chamber, where two women lay nude, their forms illuminated by the sporadic dance of flames from the fireplace.

"DiNes, you continue to evade my query," the voice echoed, a touch more stern this time, pulling at the corners of his consciousness. DiNes, his mind a whirlpool of confusion and intoxication, bellowed, "What is this incessant pestering? What do you want from me?" "The question is what do you want for yourself, what you secretly seek, DiNes? Are you willing to confront it yourself?" the voice whispered, emanating from the ethereal glow outside.

With heavy steps, DiNes ventured onto the veranda, greeted once again by the celestial beacon that seemed to be reaching out to touch his very soul. "Why are you haunting me?" DiNes demanded, a hint of desperation tainting his defiant stance. "Desires haunt, tyrannical they behave undisciplined in an unconventional way. Gnawing and pestering the soul. Stirring ravenous yearnings awaking your soul from its slumber and instigating thirst, beckoning for relief," the voice replied, its ethereal tones echoing around him. DiNes, caught between frustration and a growing sense of dread, spat defiantly, "I desire nothing, nothing at all, all I desire I have acquired."

"Your stubborn denial cannot mask the true nature of your quest, DiNes," the celestial entity persisted, its voice tinged with a nurturing yet stern resonance. "You are trapped in a cycle of superficial satisfaction, a futile attempt to fill the gaping void within you." DiNes, his facades crumbling, protested weakly, "I haven't called upon you. I haven't asked for this soul-searching voyage."

The celestial entity persisted, its voice now almost maternal, urging him to look beyond his self-imposed blindness. "DiNes, delve deep within your psyche," The voice instructed. "Who's blind?" DiNes countered in another futile attempt to argue. As the celestial dialogue unfolded, DiNes was gradually stripped of his pretense, leaving him exposed and vulnerable under the scrutiny of the ethereal presence. In a moment of heartbreaking realization, DiNes murmured, his voice trembling, "I don't know... I truly don't know what I am seeking." As before, the star receded, leaving DiNes alone, a figure grappling with the shards of his crumbling self-perception. That night, he remained motionless, his mind wrestling with the potent question that threatened to undo him.

As dawn arrived, a bewildered DiNes returned to his chamber, a storm of determination and fury brewing within him. "Get up! Get out, now!" he thundered, his voice echoing with a newfound authority. The women startled, hurried to dress. One attempted to placate him with sultry words and gestures, but DiNes was past the point of being swayed by superficial allure. "Silence! Leave, before I lose what little control I have left and have you physically thrown out," he roared, storming towards the lavatory, a torrent of conflicting emotions raging within him. Seizing the opportunity, the women hastily adorned themselves, their fear mingled with an opportunistic streak. With swift and experienced hands, one pilfered DiNes money clip, her face a mask of disdain and opportunism. "Let's get out of this pitiful place," she urged her companion, their arms interlocked as they hurriedly abandoned the scene of their nightly escapade.

Chapter Two

"Encounters"

For weeks that stretched long and lonely, DiNes sought solitude. His imposing manor echoed with the absence of guests, the quietude disrupted only by the rhythmic crashing of waves from the nearby beach, where he often wandered, haunted by the celestial voice that seemed to have forsaken him. During one of these introspective sojourns, a figure caught his eye: a woman sitting gracefully upon a large rock, her silhouette set against the rising moon. She was engrossed in the simple act of throwing pebbles into the water, a serene picture of contemplation that momentarily caught him off guard.

He approached her cautiously, the flicker of curiosity replacing his usual arrogance. "You seem lost in thoughts," he remarked, trying to ease into a casual conversation. The woman glanced over her shoulder, her eyes twinkling with an enigmatic charm. "Isn't the shore the perfect place to lose oneself in contemplation?" she replied with a knowing smile. As the conversation unfurled, a strange dance of words and ego ensued. DiNes, taken aback by her ignorance of his fame, prodded further, his curiosity piqued and his pride slightly wounded. But the woman remained unperturbed, her aura one of genuine simplicity and unpretentious wisdom.

She shared fragments of her life nothing to personal - her regular visits from France, her responsibilities towards her blind father, her tragic loss of her husband. With each word, DiNes found himself drawn more towards her grace than her physical beauty, which seemed to defy the passage of time. She bore her maturity like a crown, enhancing her allure, grounding her in a reality far removed from DiNes erstwhile hedonistic world. As DiNes pressed his company onto her, the strange aura of desperation and longing clinging to him seemed to wither in the face of her calm rejection. "Are you sure you don't want me to stay and accompany you, the shore can be quite overtaking in the evening. I wouldn't want you to get frighten out here alone", DiNes persuaded her. However, his persuasion only annoyed her; she felt his invasion of her solitude was in impertinence. Her preference for solitude, for a quiet conversation with herself over his famed companionship, stung him in places he didn't know could hurt.

"Most women would have gladly taken me up on my offer "DiNes boasted and sulked at the same time. "Hum I am certain they would have," she replied and then, she offered him a piece of wisdom, a lesson disguised as a casual remark, a gentle nudge towards introspection and authenticity. "True conversations happen when we are alone, for then we converse with our souls, undiluted and honest," she said, her gaze fixed on the undulating waves, a mirror to her tranquil soul. DiNes found himself disarmed, his well-rehearsed lines of persuasion and charm falling flat in the face of her self-assured grace. As she stood to leave, a sudden sense of loss gripped him, making him reach out almost desperately. "May I know your name?" he called out, his voice echoing the vulnerability that seemed to have crept into his core. She paused, turning slightly, her smile a blend of mystery and promise. "All in good time." When the stars align, our paths will cross again," she assured, leaving DiNes standing amidst the moonlit waves, a lone figure grappling with questions that seemed to pierce deeper with each encounter, tearing away layers of his facade, nudging him towards a truth he had long ignored.

As her figure merged with the shadows, DiNes remained his mind a whirlpool of conflicting emotions and dawning realizations. For the first time, he found himself questioning his worth beyond his fame, his substance beyond his riches. And thus, amidst the symphony of waves and whispers of the night breeze, DiNes embarked on a journey inward, a journey to find answers that lay buried within, a journey to rediscover the man lost amidst the dazzle of riches and false adorations.

Two weeks later DiNes's sat alone at his vast mansion, which once echoed with laughter and lavish parties, felt oddly silent. As the flames danced in the fireplace, illuminating the grandeur of the foyer, DiNes found himself lost in thoughts of the enigmatic woman from the beach. Her words and wisdom seemed to have marked him, steering his thoughts away from his usual desires. A sudden intrusion brought him back to reality. "Excuse me Master DiNes, I hate to interrupt your solitude, however, the Mandu's are in the foyer and they will not take no for an answer, they insist on meeting with you this eveni -, "Before Charles could finish his sentence his long-time acquaintances, the Mandu's, stood before him. "I beg your pardon!" Charles exclaimed. The Mandu's had made their own way to DiNes before they could properly be escorted. "Its fine Charles I will take it from here." DiNes said excusing Charles from the room.

The aura they exuded was one he was all too familiar with—hedonism and pleasure-seeking. In earlier times, he would have welcomed such an encounter, a break from the monotony, an avenue for pleasure. But today, everything felt different. Mable's wasted no time letting her intentions be known. Her advances, which might have once stirred him, now only evoked disgust. The memory of the mysterious woman, her calm demeanor and profound words, juxtaposed with the scene unfolding before him, made him realize the hollow nature of his past indulgences.

As the scandalous scene unfurled in front of him, a part of DiNes recoiled. Mable, with a flick of her wrist, unbuttoned her halter, her bare torso now demanding attention in the soft glow of the firelight. DiNes stammered, feeling an awkward mixture of irritation and distress, "Mable, this... this isn't right. Not tonight." Mable paused, her eyes flickering with confusion and annoyance. "What's gotten into you, DiNes? You've never refused an adventure before," she purred, trying to regain her control over the situation. Franklin chimed in, his voice slightly slurred from the alcohol, "Come now, DiNes. Don't be such a bore. Mable has been quite looking forward to this." But DiNes felt an unmistakable repulsion at Franklin's leering gaze, a revulsion he had never acknowledged before. Mabel dropped to the floor and began crawling towards DiNes with and evil seductive look in her eyes. DiNes could see the reflection from the flames in her pupils. Mabel continued crawling until she found herself DiNes's lap, with both hands stretched in front of her she started unbuttoning his pants. DiNes felt trapped and aroused at the same time it was all happening to fast, before he knew it he stood up abruptly, causing Mable to fall to the floor, he exclaimed, "No, I told you not now, not ever. I can't continue like this!" Mable picked herself up, her face a mask of fury and embarrassment. "How dare you, you're refusing me? So, what now, huh DiNes? Turning into a prude suddenly, are we?"

DiNes shook his head, his voice filled with a newfound determination, "No, Mable. Not a prude. Just someone who seeks higher ground and sick of this cesspool, now fix yourself and get out, you and that ridiculous drunkard of a thing you call husband." Franklin laughed mockingly, staggering slightly as he took another swig from his glass. "Cesspool you say? Oh, please. Spare us the sudden moral high ground, DiNes. We've all enjoyed the pleasures of the flesh equally." "As far as I recall Franklin YOU haven't enjoyed anything but a drink in the last 20 years, your pockets might be rich and full but your equipment is broke and empty." DiNes retorted. The room grew tense as DiNes' face hardened. He looked at them, truly looked at them, and felt a great chasm had grown between them. It was as if the scales had fallen from his eyes, revealing the sordid truth of their relations. "I'm sorry, no need to trade insults," DiNes finally said, his voice quieter now, yet resolute. "I cannot be part of this anymore. Please, leave." Mable scoffed, hastily pulling her dress back on. "Fine! Have it your way. Come on, Franklin. Let's leave this sanctimonious fool to his 'meaningful' pursuits."

As the couple exited, leaving behind a trail of disappointment and disillusionment, DiNes couldn't help but feel an unexpected surge of relief. The break from his past was painful, yet necessary. For the first time in years, DiNes felt an inkling of self-respect, a desire to break free from the chains of debauchery that had held him captive for so long.

Alone in the silence that followed, DiNes sank into his chair, overwhelmed by the magnitude of the change that was beginning within him. Unable to get the image of the look on Mable's face as she desperately attempted to lure him into her and Franklin's bottomless culvert. How had he allowed himself to sink so low to become a part of such an evil demoralizing Ménage A Trios? Who was Franklin to try and convict him, why, how could a man allow himself to be purchased with so little price, standing there in a boy's shoes while witnessing his wife have her way with any man she pleased. It was disturbing to him, how he could have participated in such debasing behavior, no wonder he and Franklin sought any means of mental escape they could get their hands on. Tonight, he vowed to himself, that he would never again lay eyes on the pair. He had a good mind to refund the Mandu's all that they paid him for his courtesan services over the years.

11

He allowed himself a few moments to mourn for the person he once was, a person so entangled in the allure of hedonism that he lost sight of his own values. DiNes palmed his face in shame, what would his late mother think of him. The women on at the shore crept back into his mind. His mind echoed with the serene voice she possessed, her words now striking a profound chord within him. "When we are alone, we can hear our thoughts; we are prompted to have integrity with our thoughts and be true to ourselves." She had been like a mirror reflecting back the depths of solitude he so deeply needed to explore, to rediscover the essence of who he truly was. DiNes managed to pull himself together enough to go search for Charles.

"From now on I don't want any visitors, no matter what the cause is do you hear me Charles?" DiNes snapped as he entered his quarters. "Why yes Sir, I only informed you because they said it was urgent." Charles explained. "Well moving forward no matter who shows up at this door turn them away, are you clear?" DiNes ordered again. "Yes, Sir as clear as crystal," Charles replied. DiNes retired to his bed chambers furious. He couldn't quite understand his fury that entered into him again. It was the mere mention of the Mandu's. *"How did I ever allow myself to become involved with them"* DiNes spoke out loud.

"Because you wanted your rewards in advance, you allowed greed to consume you. Over indulging yourself without any self-control or discipline, you plunged into the abyss." A voice whispered. DiNes turn around slowly..."You're back." "Yes I am here only because you cried out for me" The voice replied. "I, I did no such thing" DiNes replied. "Surely you did, your heart cried out for me and I responded." "See here I am strong I need no one, I never cried out for you." DiNes responded in defense. "Oh but you did, your mind plays tricks on you and causes you to lie to yourself but the heart knows better, it is the real source of truth in you and it cries for justice for righteousness and for redemption." The voice countered. "So let's say that I or my heart has called out to you, what is it asking for?" DiNes asked frustrated with the vague answers that seem to be a litany of parables.

"That is for you to tell me DiNes. "What do you want? " The voice replied. "I am not sure, there are things turning in my mind that I can't process perhaps... I, I well I don't know I, I just can't say." DiNes said as sat down on the bench at the foot of his bed placing his head in his hands. "DiNes you have the answers." The voice consoled him. "I don't I honestly don't know what I need. I have spent my whole life gaining. I never thought I was deficient of anything" DiNes said as his voice cracked. "You say that you have gained DiNes, tell me, where are the spoils from your gain?" The voice asked. "Why they are here, right here with me." DiNes replied. "Give me an inventory." The voce commanded. "I have this house, my fine garments, I have servants, I have food, the finest in transportation, and I can have any woman and any man at my beck and call. Shall I go on?" DiNes replied with confidence. "Is all that you have named obtained by your own hand and by your own desire?" The voice asked "I ah, I mean I guess so the garments were handpicked by me, my servants are legacy from my father, their salaries have all be arranged for at my father's death, but yes I have acquired them. This house was also acquired but I - I suppose it is just as good as any home I would have chosen for myself. My transportation was gifted of course but...but it is probably what I would have chosen." DiNes replied in a humble tone.

DiNes was beginning to feel vulnerable and helpless. This was a feeling he hated it reminded him of his childhood. "Where are we going with this? Why the inquisitorial? DiNes begin asking in a defensive tone. The voice was silent. "Answer ME!" DiNes shouted. The voice was yet still silent. DiNes stormed on to the veranda shouting "WHAT DO YOU WANT FROM ME!!" There was no response. DiNes's eyes brimmed with a red crimson as he looked about the sky. Exhausted DiNes sat down to calm himself. "I am losing my mind" he said to himself. Feeling compromised and foolish DiNes burst in to an uncontrolled laughter laughing hysterically he sat back in the chair with his hand covering his forehead. "I am one sick guy" DiNes said allowed as he chuckled. "No more opium for me"

When the laughter stopped DiNes sat in the chair gazing at the stars. Soon an image of the woman he met two weeks ago appeared in his mind again. He wondered when she would return again and if so would he see her. Why has she not heard of him it was odd. DiNes thought of asking around to see if any of the natives knew who she was. Ah she mentioned that her father was blind and did business on the Island. He shouldn't be that hard to find DiNes thought to himself. I know I will through a party and invite all the aristocrats and business men surely one of them will know her father. DiNes arose from his chair and headed off to bed.

12

Chapter Three

"Just What the Doctor Ordered"

Three weeks later DiNes was awakened by a disturbing commotion coming from the parlor. He could barely open his eyes as he asked himself "Am I dreaming?" He could hear a woman was screaming "Get your hands off of me, I will have you thrown in jail for assault!" "You are trespassing" Charles shouted. "Who the hell do you think you are un-hand me you fool!" The woman shouted. "Lady you are not welcome here!" Charles shouted back at her. "Leave me alone how dare you, DiNes help me where are you!" The woman shouted. DiNes groaned as he wiped his eyes and sat upright in bed. The commotion was getting louder and he knew that he was not dreaming. "What is it, what is all this commotion about?" DiNes shouted from top of the staircase. "You see I knew he was here! LET ME GO! The woman shouted even louder. "Ma'am I am warning you if you don't leave now I will have you escorted off this property! Charles shouted back at her. "I am not going anywhere, yes call the authorities I am not leaving until I know he is okay!" the woman responded with rage.

"Let her go Charles" DiNes ordered as he walked into the parlor. It was Amoremea she was enraged like a wild cat. Amoremea snatched herself away from Charles's grip tripping over her own feet and falling to the floor. "DiNes what is going on? "she sobbed. "Are you up there with some whore?" she said as she struggled to regain her composure. DiNes reached down to lift her off the floor. "No I am not, not that it is any of your concern." DiNes replied in a rather calm tone. "Why you, you, bas-"Amoremea began to say as she lifted her hand to strike DiNes's face however, DiNes caught her hand just before it reached his left cheek, with his right hand gripping tightly he pulled her close to him. "Calm down" DiNes said in a soft seductive voice smiling sheepishly at her.

Amoremea collected herself. Her dress was torn, lipstick smudged and her mascara was running profusely down her cheeks. She appeared to be something right out of a horror movie. "I instructed Charles to send all callers away. I have been in thought these last few weeks and I needed time alone," DiNes begin explaining now feeling very sorry for her. "Please go into the powder room to clean yourself up and Charles please tell Nicolette to fetch a dress for Amoremea" Amoremea staggered into the powder room mumbling to herself "crazy fools what the hell is going on around here." DiNes shook his head in disbelief thinking, "*how can I escape this mess, what grave have I dug for myself?*"

As Amoremea stepped out of the powder room, she couldn't shake off the feeling that DiNes's behavior was unusually distant. They always enjoyed each other's company - what had changed this time? She found him on the couch, immersed in the scene outside the window, seemingly unaware of her return. She took a moment to admire his handsome profile before clearing her throat to announce her presence, but he remained unresponsive.

"DiNes," she called, frustration creeping into her tone. It seemed as though he was in a trance, utterly oblivious to her calls. "DiNes, are you ignoring me?" she pressed, irritation mounting.

Suddenly roused, DiNes looked somewhat startled. "Oh, I didn't realize you were back," he stammered, clearly caught off guard.

Amoremea couldn't hold back her annoyance any longer. "I've been standing here for some time calling your name, but it seems you've chosen to ignore me," she accused, her voice rising in volume.

DiNes tried to appease her. "I'm sorry, dear. I was lost in thought, trying to sort some things out. I didn't mean to ignore you."

Her anger unabated, Amoremea shot back, "Well, do you want me here or not?"

Trying to defuse the escalating situation, DiNes implored, "Please, calm down. I can't think clearly with all this noise. It's a beautiful day; why don't you visit the market or spend some time at the beach? You always enjoy soaking up the sun, and it might help you relax." His attempt at diversion was subtle, but the underlying plea for some space was evident.

"I don't want to go to the beach, besides I have something better in mind that will surely take the edge off." Amoremea said as she moved closer. "Ah- Dear I am not sure I can perform now," DiNes said as her looked her up and down. "You'll never know until we get started. Come let us retreat to your chambers." Amoremea said seductively as she held out her hand to DiNes. DiNes stood up, took ahold of her hand and escorted her to his bed chambers. "I honestly don't know what has gotten into you, avoiding me for days and making me - Amoremea wait," Amoremea said as she turned to wrap her arms around DiNes's neck. DiNes gripped the back of Amoremea's neck and buttocks placing his mouth over her lips. He thrust his tongue inside her sweet mouth, probing in a rhythmic motion causing her to melt in his arms. The two begin tearing at each other clothes away until they found themselves in the bed in the throes of passion.

DiNes and Amoremea carried on for what seemed hours until they both collapsed from exhaustion sleeping peacefully in each other's arms. Suddenly there was a tap at the door "Excuse me Mr. VàsSon I have Ms. Amoremea's dress ready" as squeaky voice said from the other side of the door. "Mr. VàsSon are you there?" The squeaky voice continued. "huh....oh yes, yes just leave it on the door post DiNes said as he cleared his throat and tried to make since of what he was saying. "Have Charles pay you on the way out." He called out. This was a regular routine for DiNes and Amoremea. Amoremea would show up at DiNes's place with no change of clothes and DiNes would have Nicolette supply her with a change of clothing. DiNes would cover the bill upfront and later submit the bill to Amoremea either she or her benefactor would reimburse him.

Amoremea appreciated the arrangement, feeling supported and cherished by DiNes. From his end, DiNes savored the agreement too, as it allowed him to retain his wealth without redundant expenditures. He harbored a deep affection for Amoremea, enchanted by her striking beauty and the irresistible allure of her physique, attributes that she wielded with remarkable prowess. Having her grace his arm like a radiant trophy brought him an undeniable satisfaction. However, as time passed, Amoremea's high-maintenance disposition started to weigh on him, her incessant complaints draining the initial delight he found in their encounters. The intimacy they once shared, now a well-trodden path, left nothing new to explore, no surprises to ignite the initial thrill of their passionate hunt. Five years into their liaison, the spark had dimmed considerably, the electrifying charge of their early days replaced by a monotonous routine. Despite their long-standing relationship, the concept of marriage remained far removed from their shared plans, their connection teetering on the brink of familiarity's edge.

Amoremea had a benefactor that would withdraw if she were to become the wife of another and Amoremea refused to work. She wouldn't dream of living in poverty therefore this was her best option since DiNes made it perfectly clear he was not seeking marriage nor was he of marriage material. His reputation was notorious as it reeked of spirits, intoxications and promiscuity. Amoremea and her benefactor had an arrangement. Her benefactor was impotent and lived in France. Amoremea would accompany him to prestigious engagements and abroad when needed in return for her appearance he would sponsor her.

DiNes and Amoremea slept off and on well into the night waking for more rounds of deep passionate love making and food. By 11:00 PM they were both in a deep sleep. At Midnight a strong wind came and blew the French doors leading to the veranda from DiNes's bed chambers. DiNes was awakened by someone calling his name. "No more please Amoremea let us rest now." "Who are you talking to honey? I think you are talking in your sleep again" Amoremea replied in a sluggish tone. "Huh, oh okay" DiNes replied as he rolled over to continue his sleep. One hour passed when DiNes heard a loud whisper again "DiNes!" followed by what felt like a poke on his shoulder. DiNes sat erect in his bed in one swift motion throwing the covers off of his body

"WHAT!" he shouted as he looked around. Amoremea barely flinched as she grunted in her sleep. "DiNes you disappoint me" the voice said. "What are you talking about?" DiNes said and he continued to look wildly around the room wiping his eyes. "Why do you do this?" The voice rejoined, the voice as usual appeared to coming from the veranda. DiNes swung his feet on to the side of the bed circling them to feel for his pants. His toe caught the belt hook, he slid them closer and he reached down to bring them to his legs. "DiNes why so little value in life" the voice continued. DiNes tip toed on to the Veranda not wanting to wake Amoremea. He carefully closed the French doors behind him.

"What do you want from me? I am a simple man. I want no more than I can handle; life for me has been pleasurable. I don't want any complications," DiNes stated.

DiNes began to plead, growing tired of the voice that nagged him and tormented his soul. It had been weeks since this voice had visited him, and he thought he was free of it. "Simple, is that what you think life is, DiNes?" the voice inquired. "Why yes, why not? I mean, who wants complications?" DiNes answered arrogantly.

"DiNes, life is not as simplistic as you think. In life, there are obstacles a man must overcome; with every trial, there is an opportunity. You must push past your impediments, DiNes," the voice instructed. "But why? I am happy. I have all that a man could want," DiNes replied.

"You have all that others have wanted you to want. You have set no aims of your own and have become lazy and dubious. You have allowed man to rob you of your inherent gifts and talents; they lay dormant, withering away with time!" the voice shouted.

"Okay, okay, I have allowed myself to become spoiled. But that is a gift. Who can say the world is at their fingertips with no effort at all?" DiNes reasoned.

"Ha, you think the world is at your fingertips? No, you are the sole of every man's shoes. Your life is not your own; you are bought and paid for daily. The woman lying in your bed now has bought you for a price. You are but a mere puppet to her. For not even she would have you as a husband; what good are you to her? You are honey on a stick; as soon as it dissolves, it is no more."

"You insult me." DiNes said as he stood up "No more of this, I don't know why you have chosen me to pester, I need no lecture from you."

"You insult yourself, and you called upon me." The voice replied.

"I did no such thing I don't need you! My head hurts from this enigmatic conversation. What I need is for you to go away." DiNes retorted.

"Away - you wish me away? I am afraid it is not possible." The voice rejoined.

"Why not, why can't you leave me alone?" DiNes asked now disturbed. The response was alarming what was this, and why had this strange voice come to torment him. Suddenly he began to come to the realization "*I am losing my mind. What the hell am I doing on the veranda at this god forsaken hour talking to the sky like a madman?* "Tell me why you won't go away" DiNes called out again.

"Why won't who go away?" a voice inquired from behind the door. DiNes spun around to find Amoremea standing in the doorway, naked. "Why are you standing out here alone?" she asked with a hint of concern, stepping out onto the veranda. "And whom were you speaking with?" Trying to mask his irritation,

DiNes urged her back inside, "No one. You'll catch a cold. Let's go back inside."

Yet, Amoremea wasn't satisfied and pressed further, "But who were you talking to?" Growing increasingly irritated.

15

DiNes dismissed her persistent questions, "No one, alright?"

His sharp response caught her off guard, prompting her to snap back, "Hey, why are you so edgy?"

Sighing, he tried to alleviate her worries, albeit unconvincingly, "I am not. I'm just brain-weary," he admitted, running a hand through his hair. "I was just talking to myself."

Amoremea eyed him with evident concern, her voice softening, "Talking to yourself... Are you sure you're okay?" He let out a heavy sigh, his façade cracking,

"I am sure," he lied, the uneasiness clear in his eyes.

She moved closer, her touch gentle as she spoke, "I've never seen you like this. Lately, you've been isolating yourself and behaving oddly. Maybe you should talk to Doctor Stoge; it couldn't hurt."

His resistance seemed to crumble under her nurturing concern, his voice betraying a hint of vulnerability, "You think I need to? I... I haven't been feeling like myself lately. I suppose it wouldn't hurt."

Amoremea gave him a comforting smile, her voice laced with reassurance, "Sure thing, honey. I will call on him first thing in the morning."

Chapter Four

"Adverse Reactions"

"Come in, DiNes, come in. Tell me, why are you here today?" Doctor Stoge asked as he leaned forward. DiNes sat nervously on the couch and cleared his throat. "I am almost embarrassed to say," DiNes said hesitantly. "Try me," Doctor Stoge encouraged.

"Well, I don't know where to begin. I've been... I've been hearing a voice," DiNes admitted nervously.

"Hum... Hearing voices you say, are the voices instructing you to do anything specific like kill someone or harm yourself?" the doctor queried.

"Well, no, not exactly. It's a voice not voices. The voice is questioning what I truly want," DiNes confessed.

"Questioning what you want, huh? As in choices, like what you want for dinner?" the doctor repeated with a curious tone.

"Yes, well no, not like that the voice comes to me in a whisper, constantly asking me what I desire and scrutinizing my integrity, I think I'm losing my mind," DiNes elucidated.

The doctor leaned back in his chair and removed his glasses. "DiNes," he began calmly, "I don't believe you are losing your sanity. It seems you are at a juncture in your life where your conscience is beginning to weigh on you. You might have committed actions in your past that you aren't proud of, and perhaps you aspire to make amends. It also appears that you have reached a stage in your life where you yearn for more; your latent aspirations are beckoning you. Every individual encounters this phase at some point in their life. Some pursue their dreams fearlessly, while others suppress them deep within. I would advise you to chase your dreams, regardless of the potential sacrifices involved. You are at a midpoint in your life, with ample time to forge a meaningful path ahead. Sometimes the mind creates illusions that seem very real though they are only in our head. This usually happens when we consume hallucinogenic drugs, or experience a traumatic event. My guess is you are in need of a change and this voice is leading to make it. I strongly suggest you seize this opportunity and embark on a fulfilling journey. The next time the voice comes to you don't fight against it allow it to lead you" Dr. Stoge counselled.

Transitioning to another concern, Dr. Stoge inquired, "Now tell me, DiNes, have you been sleeping well?" as he opened his prescription pad.

"Well, I suppose so. I have had some sleepless nights, but for the most part, my sleep has been adequate," DiNes responded.

"I could prescribe some tranquilizers to aid in relaxation if you feel the need," Dr. Stoge proposed.

"No, I have plenty at home," DiNes declined. "However, I do have a question to ask you," DiNes said, changing the subject.

"Yes, go on," Dr. Stoge urged. "You know most of the men and women of this town, correct?" DiNes asked.

"I suppose so. Not everyone is a patient of mine, but I know a good number of them because of the social factions I belong to. Why do you ask?" Dr. Stoge replied, now curious.

"Well, I was wondering if you knew of a blind businessman who visits this island once a month or so. I know it's a long shot but it's all I have to go on?" DiNes inquired, hopeful for information.

"Indeed, I do. Mr. Sohan Pondeaux. He comes once a month, escorted around the island by his brother, Peter Pondeaux. His daughter also accompanies him. Sohan is a chemist, actually. May I ask why you're curious about him?" Dr. Stoge inquired further.

"Ah no special reason, I had just heard talk of him and was curious. A chemist, you say? How does he manage that?" DiNes probed further, his interest piqued.

"Yes, an interesting story indeed. He wasn't always blind; a hazardous chemical mishap cost him his sight. However, he remains a brilliant chemist. Once a month, he brings formulas and participates in the board meetings of the Medical Pharmacist Association here on the island. You might want to check the hospital bulletin board for the exact date of their next meeting," Dr. Stoge suggested.

"Thank you, doctor. And one more thing, do you happen to know his daughter's name?" DiNes asked, struggling to maintain a neutral expression. "Yes, her name is Magdalena," Dr. Stoge replied with a knowing smile.

"Well, doc, that's all I need. I'll settle my bill on the way out," DiNes said as he stood briskly from the chair.

"Remember, DiNes, schedule a follow-up appointment with my receptionist for two weeks from now," Dr. Stoge called after him as he exited the room.

DiNes hurried out of Dr. Stoge's office and made his way to St. Anthony's Hospital downtown. Breathless, he asked the receptionist, "Could you tell me where the bulletins for the Pharmaceutical Board meetings are posted?"

She offered a warm smile and replied, "They are down the hall in the main lobby."

Without losing a moment, DiNes darted down the hall to the main lobby. His eyes darted around before finally locating the kiosk. He approached it eagerly, scanning for the announcement of the next pharmaceutical board meeting. The details of the meeting, scheduled for the following Wednesday at 12:00 PM, seemed to leap off the board at him.

A swirl of thoughts besieged him: "Will they arrive early in the morning or perhaps Tuesday evening?" he pondered anxiously. His frustration grew, manifesting in an internal outcry: "Why can't things ever be simple?" Then, a semblance of a plan began to take shape in his mind. "I could stay on the beach both days or try to meet her at the ferry. But the exact time of her arrival is still unclear. Maybe I could check the schedule and inquire about passengers coming over from France," he mused, teetering between desperation and resolve.

With newfound determination, DiNes raced to the marina to check the ferry schedule. "Excuse me, do you have a list of the ferry schedules?" he asked the clerk. The man patiently listed the various lines before handing over a collection of schedules. DiNes, realizing he needed only the arrival times, felt a flush of embarrassment. He scrutinized the schedules, but the sheer number of arrivals seemed to complicate his plan further.

"Wow, how am I supposed to figure this out?" he muttered to himself, his hopes dwindling once again. Mumbling his thanks to the clerk, he walked away, a sinking feeling of defeat settling within him. As he distanced himself, a glimmer of resolve sparkled in his eyes. "Plan B," he whispered to himself, determination creeping back into his voice, "I will just have to wait by the beach until I see her."

That next Tuesday, DiNes waited anxiously for the evening before heading to the beach. He strolled up and down the sandy stretch, nurturing the hope and praying fervently that she would appear. DiNes paced and took rests intermittently, a routine that lasted until midnight, yet there was no sign of Magdalena. At 8:00 AM the next morning, DiNes arose, showered, dressed, prepared himself a cup of coffee, and headed to the hospital.

Arriving promptly at 11:30 AM, he proceeded to the main lobby and scrutinized the bulletin board for details of the Pharmaceutical Board meeting. "Ah, there it is—3rd floor, board room D," DiNes muttered to himself. He took the elevator to the specified floor, and upon exiting, approached a lady stationed at the receptionist desk. "Excuse me, where might I find board room D?" DiNes inquired eagerly.

The woman seemed to evaluate him for a moment before asking, "Are you a pharmacist?"

"No, but I have a friend who is, and I wanted to hand over something before the meeting begins," DiNes lied, crossing his fingers that she would let him through. After a brief pause, she replied,

"Well, the meeting doesn't start for another 20 minutes. I suppose you can go and check for him. Head straight down this hallway, take a left at the end, and it's the first door on your right."

With a quick nod of thanks, DiNes began walking swiftly down the corridor. Halfway, he halted, a sudden realization dawning upon him. "What will I say to her father when I meet him? He knows nothing about me. After five minutes DiNes devised a plan. Perhaps I could invite them to dine with me, expressing an interest in his fascinating work and a desire to learn more over dinner. Yes, that sounds plausible," DiNes reasoned with himself, resuming his brisk pace.

Soon, he found himself at the intended destination, standing before a door labelled 'Board Room D'. Heart pounding, DiNes slowly opened the door and peered inside. He spotted a group of men gathered around a table at the back, which was laden with coffee, donuts, and a few snacks. As his gaze traversed the room, he noticed an older gentleman seated at the far end of a long, Cherrywood oval table. A fedora rested on the table beside him, along with a brown folder and a white walking stick adorned with a red tip. "This has to be him," DiNes thought, inching closer with tentative steps.

"Excuse me, are you Mr. Sohan Pondeaux?" DiNes asked, clearing his throat slightly to gather some courage. The man smiled and nodded, his gaze fixated straight ahead, as if unfazed by DiNes' presence before him.

"Well, I have heard a great deal about your work through Dr. Stoge, and I must confess I am quite impressed. I was hoping to invite you to dinner to learn more about your contributions to the field," DiNes explained nervously, hoping the man would be receptive to the invitation.

"Oh? Are you a pharmacist?" Mr. Pondeaux inquired, his tone reflecting a hint of curiosity.

"No, but I was considering the possibility of opening a chemist shop and would greatly appreciate some expert advice," DiNes answered, attempting to maintain an air of confidence.

Mr. Pondeaux chuckled lightly before responding, "It sounds like you might need to gather a bit more information before embarking on such a venture. Who is your chemist? Do they reside here on the island?" DiNes felt the pressure mounting as he replied hastily,

"Ah, not exactly. He's actually based abroad."

"I trust he has graduated from a reputable medical school?" Mr. Pondeaux pressed further, his questions becoming more probing. Caught off guard, DiNes stammered,

"Yes, of course," before realizing he was venturing further into a fabricated tale that was spiraling out of control.

"And which school would that be?" Mr. Pondeaux continued, seemingly enjoying the gentle interrogation. DiNes felt his confidence waning with each passing moment, the heat rising to his face.

"I... uh, can't recall the name at the moment," he admitted, his forehead glistening with beads of sweat.

Before DiNes could further entangle himself in the web of lies he'd spun, the chairman interrupted, announcing the start of the meeting. Taking this as his cue to escape, DiNes hastily muttered, "I think it's best if we continue this conversation at a later time," before retreating from the room in a hurried pace.

Mr. Pondeaux was left in slight bewilderment, a thoughtful expression gracing his features as the room filled with the murmur of gathering attendees, all ready to commence the meeting.

"*I must be some kind of idiot*" DiNes thought to himself. I suppose I will just have to walk the beach this evening." DiNes plotted in his mind. He was growing hungry and in need of an espresso so he set out to satisfy his craving, just up the street was the Café Catalina by the shore. DiNes found himself pacing nervously outside a quaint café nestled by the seashore, a stone's throw away from the bustling market square. With a determined yet slightly desperate resolve, he made his way inside, the little bell above the door heralding his entrance. His eyes darted around; scrutinizing the early patrons, locals immersed in their morning rituals and whispered conversations.

DiNes felt like an intruder in this quiet haven, but he shook off the unease, tightening his grip on the useless ferry schedules. He approached a group of elderly men engaged in a lively discussion, their table littered with scattered newspapers and half-empty cups of coffee. DiNes seated himself at the table next to theirs. The waitress soon arrived with a glass of water and charcuterie with fresh baked bread and butter. The waitress took DiNes order and left him to his private reverie.

As DiNes sat quietly thumbing his finger on the wooden table, he overheard the men talking one of them happened to be the driver for Mr. Peter Pondeaux and mentioned that he would be driving he, his brother, and niece to dinner at the Grand DeVous around 5:00 p.m. DiNes smiled to himself "*well it seems I have found favor in the creator after all.*" DiNes's mind was now at ease as he broke off a piece of bread smeared it with butter and took a tantalizing bite. Soon he would be in front of the woman who had haunted his thoughts for weeks. The room seemed to echo with the gravity of his quest, the ticking clock on the wall marking the passage of precious minutes until his affinity would be requited.

Amidst the soft hum of conversation and the clinking of fine china at the Grand DeVous, DiNes stepped forward, his heart fluttering with a blend of nerves and hope. Handing the maître d his hat and scarf he inquired where the Pondeaux were setting. "Yes I am here to join Mr. Peter Pondeaux and party this evening." DiNes announced with confidence.

"Why yes Sir right this way" The maître d replied as he prepared to escort DiNes to the table personally.

"Oh no that won't be necessary, just point me in the direction and I will find my way." DiNes arrogantly rejoined.

"As you wish they are just behind the fountain the table to the left." The maître d said as he pointed in the direction of their table. As he approached the Pondeaux family nestled at a quiet corner table, he cleared his throat, ready to deliver his well-rehearsed speech filled with admiration and respect.

'Good evening, Mr. Pondeaux, Mr. Pondeaux, Magdalena,' DiNes began, his voice steady and warm. 'I am DiNes, a great admirer of your work, sir, and I was hoping—'

Before he could continue, a piercing shriek sliced through the calm atmosphere. DiNes froze, feeling a chill creep down his spine as he recognized the slurred voice of a woman from his past. She staggered in, her face a volatile mix of anger and intoxication. 'DiNes, you bloody spineless coward!' she yelled, her voice echoing through the silent room. The restaurant's patrons turned their faces masks of shock and disapproval.

DiNes turned slowly, his face pale, his voice barely more than a whisper. 'Catherine, this isn't the time—'

'Oh, isn't it?' she snarled, ignoring him and turning to address the Pondeaux family directly. 'You should know what kind of man he really is, consorting with young, naive women, only to cast them aside.'

Mr. Peter Pondeaux's stern face grew increasingly tight, his eyes flicking between DiNes and the enraged woman. "What is it, what's happening?" Mr. Sohan Pondeaux said as moved his head to and fro trying to use is senses to understand what was taking place.

"Papa please, don't be alarmed it will be fine," Magdalena said as she grabbed her father's hand in an effort to calm him. Magdalena's face was a canvas of shock and confusion, her gaze filled with questions that pierced DiNes more sharply than any accusation. How did he find them, was it a coincidence or was this some ill attempt to sway her and her father. Attempting to regain control of the situation,

DiNes stepped forward, his hands outstretched in a placating gesture. "Catherine, please, let's talk about this outside—"

Catherine's laugh was sharp and bitter. "Talk you say? Like you talked your way into my bed, and then out of it just as quickly?" Without warning, she grabbed a nearby glass, hurling its contents towards DiNes. But her aim was wild, and the liquid found a different target - Magdalena.

The crimson wine seeped into the fabric of Magdalena's pristine white dress, marking it with a stain that seemed too deep to ever be removed. The room held its breath, the only sound being the slow drip of wine onto the fine carpet.

"I... I am so sorry, Magdalena," DiNes stammered, his eyes filled with regret and pleading. Before Magdalena could respond, Cathrine lunged at him, a whirlwind of fury and resentment. The ensuing scuffle was a cacophony of gasps, shouts, and the shattering of a decorum that could never be repaired. In moments, the two found themselves in the lap of Mr. Sohan Pondeaux, whose shocked expression mirrored the chaos that unfolded before him.

The maître d soon arrived with two burley staff men, forcibly separating the battling duo and escorting them out into the cold night air. The doors of the Grand DeVous swung closed, leaving DiNes standing under the glaring street lights, his dreams shattered, perhaps beyond repair. His last pathetic desperate attempt to redeem himself DiNes raced around the restaurant looking through the windows until he found the window that allowed him to visibly see Magdalena, he uncle and father still sitting at the table, they appeared to remain in shock from the nights dramatics. Waiters fussed about as Magdalena frantically wiped her dress with the table napkin.

DiNes's voice cracked, broken and desperate, as he called through the window. "Magdalena, please, believe me, it's not like it seems." Magdalena just sat in shock ignoring him and focusing on the crimson that stubbornly wove its way through her dress. How had he found out her name? How dare he address her and her father as though they were mutual acquaintances? Magdalena could only imagine what questions her father would have for her, he would certainly want to know how she had come to know such a scoundrel. Come to think of it he did mention that he had heard of her father's accomplishments through Dr. Stoge, how he had come to find an interest in her father's work she wondered.

The door remained closed, and Magdalena's face was hidden, locked away behind thick oak and shattered illusions. DiNes was left alone in the cold, a solitary figure standing amidst the harsh glow, a beacon of lost opportunities and tarnished hopes.

Magdalena pondered all through the night, a faint smile crept across her face as she lay in the bed, revisiting the evening. "*He found me, he actually found me. What an impression I must have made on him.*" She had to admit DiNes did look rather dashing in his back suits and tie. She recalled the determination in his eyes as he tried to explain. Something about the way he tried to finesse the woman announcing his profligacy stirred emotions in her. Even in such a case he was charming.

Magdalena tossed and turned in her bed. "*If only he had waited until our paths crossed again none of that tomfoolery would have taken place, father and uncle might have given him a chance.*" Magdalena reconciled, she was equally disappointed for she fancied him just as much on the night they met. Her approach was quite different though, she needed time to study him and inquire of his reputation. Not to mention much of her heart was still with Lucas.

21

3

On the night of their first meeting Magdalena was full of sorrow an earlier incident caused her to recall the death of her husband Lucas. Thinking she would never fully recover enough to move on with her life, she took a night's stroll on the beach the clear her thoughts, it was there she met DiNes. That evening she contemplated joining her husband in the afterlife, DiNes's bold interruption thwarted her decision.

Magdalena supposed it was some sort of divine intervention. For weeks after their encounter he stayed on her mind. Magdalena fought hard to suppress any sort of attraction that crept into her mind. As far as she was concerned she was still a married woman. Allowing another man to enter her life felt like betrayal, confused by her thoughts and this intrusive desire for the comfort of another man only added to her guilt. However, her plans that seem to be the answer to putting an end to her agony were interrupted. Perhaps God had something else in mind. Magdalena went home that night realizing death was not the answer, the fact that she was still living and breathing had to mean something and possibly Mr. DiNes was a contributor to finding her purpose

Chapter Five

"Waking Up"

By the time DiNes arrived home, he was thoroughly exhausted. "Charles, I'm starving. Can Maria prepare a late dinner for me?" DiNes requested, his voice tinged with fatigue. Charles, attentive as always, asked, "Is there something special you would like to eat?"

"No, anything will do," DiNes replied, his energy seemingly sapped. Later, he found himself seated at the dining table, mindlessly staring at a plate of untouched food, his thoughts swirling with strategies to mend things with Magdalena. He couldn't fathom why he felt so irresistibly drawn to her. The evening ticked away as he pondered his mind racing until it could race no more.

At 7:00 p.m., just before DiNes retreated to his bedroom, a flicker of hope kindled a new plan in his mind. Perhaps he could encounter her again at the shore, maybe during a late-night stroll, just like before. Eager to act on this new strategy but hindered by a pounding headache, he decided to rest for a bit.

Navigating to his bathroom, DiNes opened the medicine cabinet and retrieved a small bottle of pills. He unscrewed the cap, dispensed three pills into his hand, and then securely replaced the bottle in the cabinet. He grabbed a paper cup from the dispenser, filled it with water from the running faucet, and swiftly gulped down the pills with the water aid.

DiNes then retreated to the sitting area, where he settled down on the couch with a magazine from the coffee table. As he leafed through the pages, his weariness overpowered him, and within 20 minutes, DiNes was enveloped in the comforting arms of sleep.

A cool wind swept through the room, causing DiNes to shiver involuntarily. Half-asleep on the couch, he realized the night had settled in deep. "Ah, what time is it?" he exclaimed, frantically searching for the light switch. Once illuminated, his anxious gaze located the clock; he blinked in disbelief, praying it was a mistake. But a glance at his watch confirmed it: 1:01 AM.

"Dammit!" DiNes shouted, his voice echoing ominously through the silence. In a flustered state, he hunted for his shoes, nearly tripping in his haste to descend the stairs. Bursting out the door, he sprinted towards the shore, desperation fueling his steps. His breath became ragged as he scoured the shoreline, a growing realization that he might not find Magdalena gnawing at him. After a fruitless hour, he retreated home, a shadow of his earlier fervor.

Back in his chambers, DiNes ventured onto his veranda, his face upturned to the heavens as he sighed heavily. "Why... why... why..." he murmured to the uncaring stars. A sudden voice pierced the stillness. "You know why. YOU ARE NOT READY!" Taken aback, DiNes replied, somewhat sardonically, "I was wondering when you'd show up. So humor me, what am I not ready for?"

"I never left. I've been right here waiting on you," the voice echoed, tinged with a solemnity that seized DiNes' attention. He mumbled a defeated "Here we are back to parables again. Oh well whatever you say", weariness seeping into his bones. "DiNes, you are not ready for her. Tonight, you sought love while harboring the very poison that could jeopardize any potential future with her," the voice imparted wisdom wrapped in enigma. DiNes, now too exhausted to engage in philosophical discourse, merely murmured, "I see", before abandoning the veranda. The comfort of his bed embraced him as he collapsed onto it, the world fading as he succumbed to a deep, much-needed sleep.

The morning sun sneaked through the blinds of DiNes's bedroom, playfully teasing his eyelids open. As the orchestra of birds heralded a new day with lively chirps, the enticing aroma of freshly brewed coffee seemed to have hands gently coaxing him out of bed.

He sat up, motivation sparkling in his eyes. "That's it! I got it! I know exactly what I must do" he exclaimed, a solution crystallizing in his mind. With purpose in his step, he moved to the bathroom, the mantra "I know what I have to do" reverberating in his mind as he attended to his morning rituals.

Awhile later, he descended the stairs to the inviting scent of coffee in the kitchen. Maria greeted him with her ever-present warmth, her eyes twinkling with joy as she asked, "Would you like some breakfast, Mr. VàsSon?"

Caught in a whirlpool of thoughts yet managing a sincere smile, he replied, "Absolutely, Maria. How about two eggs, two patties of sausage, half an avocado, some buttered toast, and jam?"

Maria giggled at his hearty request, teasing, "Well, someone's got a big appetite this morning!" He chuckled, "Indeed, I'm famished!" He then retreated to his study, returning with a pen and notepad in tow. As he settled on the patio, bathed in the golden embrace of the sun, he said, "I'll be having breakfast here, Maria. The morning is just too beautiful to ignore."

As he scribbled fervently onto the notepad, Maria approached, a tray bearing his sizable breakfast in her hands. "Would a fresh cup of coffee accompany the meal well, Mr. VàsSon?" she inquired, her voice brimming with enthusiasm.

DiNes paused, offering her a warm smile, "You know, I think I've had my fair share of caffeine for today. Could I have some freshly squeezed orange juice instead?"

With a lively "Yes, sir!" Maria disappeared into the kitchen, her humming providing a melodious backdrop to the scribbling sounds of the pen dancing across the paper.

After breakfast, DiNes stood, his notepad filled with pages of fresh ideas tucked under his arm. He collected his dishes, surprising Maria as he appeared in the kitchen.

"Oh Mr. VàsSon, I could have taken care of that!" she exclaimed, a hint of mock reprimand in her tone.

He grinned, patting her gently on the back, "I know, Maria, but I didn't mind." As he turned to leave,

Maria called, "Lunch plans, Mr. VàsSon? Any preferences?"

He paused at the threshold, throwing a thoughtful glance over his shoulder, "Surprise me, Maria!" His voice echoed through the house, carrying a newfound enthusiasm and determination as he vanished up the stairs, ready to embrace the day's possibilities.

DiNes transitioned from the warm glow of morning inspiration to decisive action. After selecting a crisp outfit for the day, he swiftly moved to the bathroom for a refreshing shower. The hot water rejuvenated him, setting a determined tone for the day. Once dressed, he strode purposefully to his study, retrieved the deed to his house, and called out for Charles... "Charles!" DiNes projected firmly.

Charles appeared promptly, displaying his usual attentive demeanor. "Yes, sir, how may I assist you?"

DiNes handed over a two page list to Charles with a composed but serious expression. "Charles, I'm stepping out for a few hours. I need you to go through this list and contact everyone on it. Let them know I intend to settle my accounts and find out the exact amounts I owe them. Also I have listed three individuals on the second page for which, I owe nothing however I wish to refund all that they have bestowed upon me. I expect a detailed report upon my return."

With an acknowledging nod, Charles took the list. DiNes, not waiting for a verbal response, turned on his heels and left for his car. At exactly 12:00 PM, he arrived at his destination, the bank.

DiNes approached the counter confidently. "I need to speak with a loan officer, preferably Jon Raè if he's available," he requested the bank teller, his tone carrying an undercurrent of urgency.

The teller blinked at the abrupt request but quickly regained her composure. "Uh, let me check Mr. Jon Raè's availability for you," she said, busying herself with the system. A few clicks later, she lifted the receiver and dialed Jon Raè's extension. "May I have your name, please?"

"DiNes VàsSon," he supplied, maintaining his poised demeanor.

After a brief conversation over the phone, the teller hung up and directed DiNes to the waiting area. "Please have a seat in the lobby, Mr. VàsSon. Mr. Jon Raè will be with you shortly." DiNes nodded and retreated to the designated area, the deed to his house clutched firmly in his hand. As he reviewed the document, a whirlpool of memories threatened to consume him. As DiNes revisited these memories, he realized the true extent of the scars that marred his family. His upbringing in the mansion was a tapestry of joy and sorrow, love and abandonment. His father always away on business and his mother trying to busy herself as if she didn't acknowledge his absents.

Too many times DiNes passed by her room only to hear her weeping sorrowfully into her pillow. Special events like birthday's and even holidays his father was absent. He recalled hearing his mother make futile pleas for his father to stay longer when he would return, only to have them dismissed. DiNes grew up thinking this was the way of the home, fathers were simply not available they only supplied means.

Some years later his mother died from cancer it was then that his father tried to make amends, DiNes ignored his attempts just as his father did his mother when she was alive. As he prepared to start a new chapter in his life, DiNes vowed to learn from the past, to build a future that echoed the love and warmth that his mother had showered upon him, and to leave behind the bitterness that had haunted his father's steps.

DiNes might have gone on building his new constitution in his mind but he was suddenly pulled back to reality when he heard his name.

"DiNes! It's been ages!" A friendly voice called out. DiNes looked up to find, a compact man with a gleaming bald head and sharp glasses, extending a hand towards him. With a smile that melded both relief and urgency, DiNes rose and shook Jon Raè's hand firmly.

"I'm here to discuss a property matter, Jon Raè. It's quite urgent." Understanding seemed to flicker in Jon Raè's eyes.

"Of course, DiNes. Please, step into my office, and we'll sort it out."

DiNes began explaining his plans of selling the mansion. Jon Raè listened attentively. When DiNes was finished he handed Jon Raè the deed to his property. Jon Raè looked the deed over shaking his head. "It's a shame I remember this property very well. I 'm sure you had your fun as a child discovering all the back chambers and secret passages that led to the outer cove.

"Outer cover, I've no knowledge of such a thing and I've lived in this house my entire life." DiNes replied with a puzzled look on his face.

"Yes Sir there are secret passages throughout the house come let me show you." Jon Raè as stood up from his desk moving toward the file cabinets to retrieve the blueprints of the home. Once he found the blue prints he spread them wide on his desk for DiNes see.

"See here DiNes," Jon said as he pointed out all the hidden passages of the house. In light of the new news DiNes decided to take a few more days to think about selling the mansion.

"Please Jon if you could give me a few more days, I'd like some time to investigate this." Mean time if you don't mind can you determine what the mansion is worth now?"

"With pleasure" Jon Raè replied before ending the meeting.

Chapter Six

"Secrets Lurking in the Depths"

The conversation with Jon Raè had unsettled DiNes, awakening an inkling of childhood curiosity that had long been buried. A secret within his own home, a vestige of his father's past - it all seemed like a tale spun from the novels he'd once loved as a boy. But the blueprint Jon had given him felt solid and real in his hands, a tangible testament to the mystery that beckoned him from just beneath his feet.

Jon Raè was an experienced realtor, having orchestrated numerous high-profile transactions throughout his career. Yet, the VàsSon estate held a particular fascination for him, steeped in whispered rumors and shadowy legends that surrounded the VàsSon lineage. And now, it seemed DiNes was on the cusp of uncovering a piece of that history, a piece that had been carefully concealed for generations.

DiNes spread the blueprint out on the grand oak table in the library, the lines and markers stark against the aging parchment. His eyes traced the labyrinthine tunnels, stretching like veins beneath the grandiose structure of his family home, reaching towards the churning waves of the sea that bordered the sprawling estate.

It felt like an omen, this discovery, a sign perhaps that there were still secrets to be uncovered, truths to be faced. As DiNes sat in the quietude of the library, the weight of his lineage seemed to press upon him, urging him to delve deeper, to seek out the hidden facets of his family history that lurked in the tunnels below.

With a resolute breath, DiNes knew he couldn't face the shadows alone. The comforting, wise presence of Charles seemed like a beacon of light in the uncertainty that lay ahead. Perhaps, DiNes thought, Charles could be his anchor, his guide in the darkness that seemed to call to him from the depths.

"Charles, there's something I need to show you." DiNes called out summing Charles to the study.

Charles entered, his demeanor radiating a calm steadiness that seemed to fill the room. As DiNes recounted his conversation with Jon and unveiled the blueprint, Charles leaned in, his eyes scanning the intricate lines and pathways, a hint of recognition flickering in his gaze.

Charles (with a hint of concern): "I had heard whispers, tales of secret passages and hidden chambers, but I never knew the extent... This place holds more secrets than we could have imagined. All my time here DiNes I have only ventured in rooms that were visible as far as service to your family and of course my quarters."

DiNes looked at Charles, a plea in his eyes, a request for guidance and support. Charles met his gaze, a silent pact forming between them, a promise to face the lurking shadows together.

Perusing the blueprints together they determined where the secret passages were located, in fact one in the very room they occupied. Together, they ventured into the depths of the VàsSon estate, flashlights piercing through the darkness as they navigated the twisting tunnels. The air was thick with the scent of damp earth and the distant roar of the sea echoed through the hollow passages.

With every step, the history of the VàsSon family seemed to pulse around them, the walls whispering tales of secrets kept and deeds obscured by time. As they ventured deeper, a strange anticipation built within DiNes, a sense that he was on the cusp of a revelation that could alter his perception of his family, and perhaps, his own identity. Frighten by what they might find on this venture, DiNes pondered if they should just leave well enough alone.

As they reached the end of the tunnels, a hidden chamber opened up before them, a sanctuary that bore the marks of his father's presence, a place where time seemed to have stood still. The artifacts and relics within spoke of a man consumed by a relentless pursuit, a pursuit that had driven him to conceal this part of his life even from his own family.

And there, in the midst of it all, DiNes found an old journal, the pages filled with his father's handwriting, a testament to the journey that had led him to this hidden sanctum, to the secrets that lay concealed within the depths of the VàsSon estate. As DiNes leafed through the journal, he realized that this discovery held the power to reshape his understanding of his past, to forge a new path forward, guided by the revelations that lay within these hidden pages.

The journey into the depths had revealed more than hidden tunnels and secret chambers; it had unearthed the complexity of his father's life, a tapestry of ambition, passion, and loss. He and Charles stood together in astonishment.

"Hand me that shovel" Charles commanded. Charles recognized something protruding from the ground. Hesitantly DiNes did as he ordered. Charles began digging soon revealed a chest of some sort, after a while it was fully visible a 6 foot by 4 inch deep metal chest. Now fully visible to both DiNes and Charles's, the two lifted it from out of the ground with every muscle in their body. Grunting and heavy panting the two were finally able to remove it from the ground. It had a padlock on it, with what little strength DiNes had left in him he used the shovel to knock the padlock off, the lock came off with ease for the latch had rusted from the damp grounds.

When the lock was finally off DiNes opened the chest, the stench was so powerful, the putrid odor quickly infiltrated the cave causing both Charles and DiNes to gag. On the very top was sackcloth filled with dead frogs. DiNes's father had placed them there as a deterrent in the event someone else discovered the treasure chest. DiNes coughing and covering his nose pulled the sack cloth from the chest and drug it out of the cave. Underneath it were captain's logs a good mound of them. Charles helped to remove them. The two took turns digging through the chest and running out of the cave to get air. Finally almost at the bottom were sleek thin bricks of gold. 30 to be exact each had a symbol of a flag and crest with the letters LE inscribed on them.

DiNes and Charles looked at each other, their eyes widening in astonishment. They had stumbled upon what seemed to be a long-lost treasure, one that bore the enigmatic initials "LE". DiNes felt the surge of a million questions racing through his mind, but the gravity of the find left him momentarily speechless. Charles, with years of wisdom etched onto his face, seemed to be taking in the magnitude of their discovery with a quieter kind of shock. He lifted one of the golden bricks, its weight substantial in his hands. The flag and crest etched on the bricks hinted at a story that stretched far back in history, a narrative intertwined with adventures at sea, possibly piracy, and hidden treasures.

With a shivering hand, DiNes reached out to touch one of the bricks. The cold gold felt surreal against his skin. It seemed that the VàsSon mansion had been safeguarding a secret far grander than anything he could have imagined. His mind raced to piece together the fragments of his family history, to decipher the role his father had played in this hidden chapter of their lineage.

DiNes (with a voice filled with wonder and confusion): "Charles, what do you make of this? Do these symbols or the initials ring any bells?"

Charles took a moment, his eyes scanning over the intricacies of the crests and the flag etched onto the bricks. He seemed to be lost in deep contemplation, sifting through years of knowledge and memory. Charles (with a voice that hinted at recognition): "I can't be certain, DiNes, but these symbols... they remind me of the markings of the old L'Équipage fleet, a group of privateers who operated under the royal banner many centuries ago. They were known to have amassed great wealth, but their operations were shrouded in mystery and controversy."

DiNes felt a chill run down his spine, the tendrils of history wrapping around him, drawing him into a narrative that seemed both fantastical and daunting. Together, they decided to retrieve the logs and leave the gold bricks, concealing the chest once more beneath the sackcloth of dead frogs. As they emerged from the cave, the weight of their discovery hung heavily between them, a secret that bound them together in ways they could not yet fully comprehend.

Back at the mansion, in the dim glow of the library's antique lamps, they pored over the captain's logs, their hands brushing over inked entries that spoke of voyages, conflicts, alliances, and treasures accumulated through dubious means. The logs hinted at connections to royalty, at deals forged in the shadows, and at the immense wealth that had been amassed by the L'Équipage fleet. DiNes felt his world tilting on its axis, the foundations of his identity shifting with each revelation. It seemed his family's history was steeped in intrigue and secrets that went far beyond the walls of their family estate. The riches they had found hinted at a legacy that was both formidable and fearsome, one that held the power to redefine everything DiNes had known about his lineage. And as DiNes and Charles delved deeper into the mysteries unraveling before them, they realized that they stood at the threshold of a journey that would take them far beyond the confines of the VàsSon estate, into the uncharted waters of history, legacy, and perhaps, redemption.

DiNes retreated to the study, his heart a tumultuous sea of both hope and doubt. The amber glow from the fireplace cast elongated shadows on the rich mahogany that lined the room, the crackling of the fire playing a melancholy symphony that resonated with the turmoil in his heart. He sank into the plush armchair, a glass of aged whisky in hand, the golden liquid dancing with the flames' reflection. The enormity of recent discoveries weighed heavily on him, pulling at the tenuous strings of hope that had begun to sprout within him, fostering dreams of a future with Magdalena. His thoughts swirled, mingling with the rich aroma of aged books and polished wood. The uncertainty surrounding the gold, the lingering memories of his father, and the fragile thread connecting him to Magdalena - everything was converging into a vortex of overwhelming complexity. Just as the flames in the hearth seemed to mirror the flickering uncertainty in his heart, the soft creaking of the door broke his reverie. Charles entered, the trusted old servant who had been a silent witness to the many phases of DiNes's life.

Charles entered with a concerned expression: "Sir, you seem to be lost in deep thought. I hope I'm not intruding." DiNes (shaking his head and offering a faint smile):

"Not at all, Charles. Your company is always a comfort." Charles hesitated momentarily before venturing further into the room, an apparent burden in his eyes. He seemed to be grappling with memories from the past, fragments of whispered conversations, and clandestine meetings that were resurfacing after all these years.

Charles sighed heavy: "Sir, there's something I've been meaning to tell you. About your father and a man named Priviot. They had a business relationship many years ago. I always found it rather strange, their hushed meetings, the gravity in their tones."

DiNes leaned forward, absorbing every word: "Go on, Charles." Charles (visibly struggling to piece together the fragments of the past):

"I recall your father working tirelessly on a project for Priviot. Those were the days when your father would lock himself in his study for hours, pouring over documents and blueprints." DiNes's heart raced as he listened, pieces of a puzzle slowly coming together, potentially offering a path to unravel the mystery surrounding the gold and his father's secretive nature.

DiNes pondered it a bit; bring his hand to his chin gently stroking it, "Do you think this project could somehow be linked to the gold we found, Charles?"

Charles paused, and then nodded: "It might very well be, Sir. It seemed to have held great significance, and perhaps... perhaps it might be a key to understanding your father's true intentions." DiNes felt a sense of resolve crystallizing within him. This could be the key to a new beginning, a chance to redeem his name and pave a path to a brighter future, one where he could stand beside Magdalena, unburdened by the sins of the past, turning him in to a hero, offering retribution to the rightful owners of the gold.

DiNes clenched his fist, determination sparkling in his eyes: "Then I have to delve deeper into this, uncover the truth that's been buried for far too long. Charles, will you stand with me in this?"

Charles (with a firm, assuring nod): "Always, Sir, to the very end." And thus, in the flickering glow of the fireplace, amidst the whispers of the night, a pact was forged - a vow to seek out the truth, to restore what was lost to an unknown victim, putting an end to secrets kept for far too long.

As the dawn of a new day stretched its golden tendrils across the horizon, DiNes, now fueled with purpose and determination, started his search for more of his father's journals. Charles joined him, and together, they scoured every nook and cranny of the sprawling mansion, a place that had transformed from a house of painful memories to a treasure trove of secrets waiting to be unveiled. In the dusty attic amidst stacks of forgotten belongings and remnants of a time long past, DiNes stumbled upon a moth-eaten box. Inside, amidst various belongings, lay the journal, an unassuming leather-bound book that had silently harbored secrets that spanned decades. DiNes carefully thumbed through the brittle pages, his eyes scanning the meticulous entries that documented his father's thoughts, projects, and dealings. The room was charged with a silent expectancy, every word revealing a layer of the intricate tale that was his father's life, a story of ambition, perhaps betrayal, and a mystery that ran deeper than the ocean that surrounded the island.

Towards the end of the journal, tucked in the creases of the binding, was a weathered note. DiNes unfolded it carefully, revealing a scrawled message from Mr. Priviot. [*Winston, I know this past year has been a torment for you, I am sorry I'm not able to make myself more available to you. However, Chantel has become ill and I myself am not up to par. Ever since ...well you know. If you wish to conclude on this matter Contact David Barclay in France, he'll know what to do.*] The room felt suddenly heavy, the air thick with the weight of discoveries yet to come. Charles watched as DiNes absorbed the contents of the note, his expression a complex dance of surprise, hope, and curiosity.

DiNes (his voice tinged with awe): "It seems like the path is leading us to France, Charles. To see a man named David Barclay...I wonder who he is and what role he plays in all of this."

Charles with a thoughtful frown: "It sounds like a new lead, Sir. Perhaps this Barclay person holds the answers we seek." DiNes nodded, his heart a turbulent whirlpool of emotions. He realized that unraveling the past was not just about clearing his father's name or bringing resolve to unclaimed gold, but also about building a future where the darkness of the past couldn't reach.

As he stood up, the journal clutched tightly in his hands, he felt a strange connection to his father, a bond that seemed to transcend time, beckoning him to uncover the truth that lay buried, yet very much alive. DiNes (his voice firm with resolve): "Charles, we have a journey ahead of us. A journey that promises to be anything but easy. But we must undertake it, for the truth, I don't believe my father would harbor spoils from ill-gotten means but I must be certain. Perhaps this is why mother suffered his absence all those years, God I pray it wasn't for sinister reasons. She suffered in silence not even in her last months was he available, it was only on her death bed did he hold her hand while she took her last breaths. This is for her retribution and for the hope of a new beginning."

Charles (his eyes twinkling with an adventurous spark): "And for the possibility of redemption, Sir."

DiNes smiled, the flickering flame of hope igniting stronger within him, fueled by the prospects of resolution and the sweet promise of reclamation that seemed to linger on the horizon, shimmering in the golden hues of the rising sun. With determined strides, DiNes left the attic, the note from Mr. Priviot securely tucked away, a beacon that hopefully lead them through a labyrinthine journey, where shadows of the past would finally give way to the light of truth.

"Oh Sir there is one matter of business I almost forgot to address with you, will you excuse me for a moment while I go and retrieve it?" Charles said as he exited the study. Upon his return he handed DiNes the list he had given him earlier. "Here you are Sir, all is accounted for."

DiNes scrutinized the list carefully. "This looks thorough, Charles. I appreciate your diligence. I'll tackle this first thing in the morning if time permits." The two exchanged nods, signaling the close of their business for the evening.

As DiNes retreated to his chambers, he took another glance at the list, specifically the second page. As he carefully reviewed it there were comments next to each name. "Refused to comply," each remark read. He mused, somewhat ruefully, "It appears that not even money can mend certain breaches." Reflecting on the untouched gold, DiNes wondered if its long dormancy was a testament to the unresolved pains of the past.

"I suppose this is when integrity takes over." DiNes murmured to himself, placing the list on his nightstand and settling on the edge of the bed. Just before retiring for the evening, he recalled something else that had slipped through his initial scrutiny of his father's journal: mentions of dealings with his paternal grandfather, something involving property and an unused dowry. DiNes's mother hailed from Scotland, UK, and their marriage had been arranged long before their births. The possibility that the gold might somehow be connected lingered in his thoughts as he finally closed his eyes.

Chapter Seven

"Business First"

In the grand study of the VàsSon mansion, the grandeur of which seemed almost out of place given the simple, almost quaint nature of the island, DiNes took a long, contemplative look at the vast room. The towering shelves filled with books of lore, history, and personal journals, the vast windows overlooking the gardens, and the centuries-old oak desk where many decisions had been made. It was here that he had decided to sell the mansion, but now, the unfolding mysteries had instilled a sense of purpose, a mission that linked him to the past and beckoned him to a future filled with untold discoveries.

One evening, as the sun painted the sky with hues of gold and crimson, DiNes sat in his favorite armchair by the fireplace, the warmth of the flames juxtaposed with the cool sea breeze drifting in from the open balcony doors. He was lost in thought, contemplating the journey he had embarked upon, when Charles entered the room, holding a tray with two glasses of the finest scotch, aged almost as long as the mysteries they were unraveling.

Charles cleared his throat, pulling DiNes out of his reverie. "Sir, I - I just got a call from Jon Raè, he says he has a price for this residence and perhaps a potential buyer. "Any thoughts on it?"

DiNes took a deep breath, "Charles, I guess I should have been honest with you, I was thinking of selling this place and moving on. These last few months have driven me to seek new horizons. I made plans to settle you and Maria with an impeccable reference. But with all that's transpiring, I believe selling the mansion now would be premature. There's so much left to uncover, and I have a strong feeling we're only scratching the surface."

Charles nodded, pouring the amber liquid into the glasses. "And what about Maria and me? You had plans..."

DiNes cut him off with a raised hand, "Those plans are on hold as well, my friend. I realized that in these trying times, I need people I trust by my side. And there are very few I trust as much as you and Maria." I am sorry if I made you feel easily dispensable, you're not neither of you, it is I who felt I didn't deserve you and was willing to run off like some wounded puppy to lick my wounds. That's over now and if in the future I do plan to sell I will include you long before I talk to anyone understood?"

A smile tugged at Charles's lips, "Understood! Well, Sir, we're in it for the long tow, then. Together." The two men raised their glasses in a silent toast. The journey they had embarked upon was no ordinary one, and they knew that the road ahead was riddled with challenges. But with trust, friendship, and unwavering determination, they were ready to face whatever awaited them. Charles handed DiNes the written phone message from Jon Raè a reminder of a decision that was, for now, on hold. The mansion, with its myriad secrets, stood tall, its walls echoing tales of the past and whispers of the adventures yet to come.

As the two sat in contemplative silence, sipping their double malt, DiNes found his mind revisiting the thoughts that had occupied him the night before. "Charles, do you remember the day my maternal grandfather visited, and he and my father had that bitter quarrel? I couldn't have been more than 12 years old at the time."

Charles shifted in his chair, setting his glass down, and took a moment to reflect before responding, "Why yes, Sir, I do. Your grandfather vowed he'd never return, and he certainly kept that promise. I remember something else too — it shattered your mother's heart, as if she hadn't already endured enough."

"Charles, do you recall what the argument was about?" DiNes inquired.

"Not really, Sir. I wasn't in the habit of eavesdropping. Once the argument started, I made myself scarce. I do remember your mother contemplating leaving the mansion afterward. What changed her mind I'm not sure—perhaps taking you away from your father. I wish I had more for you, but that's all I can recall. Your father never discussed such matters with me. My father was more of a confidant to your father and grandfather than I." Charles settled back in his chair, taking another sip of scotch and reminiscing about that day.

"Hmm, I'm just wondering if... if possibly that is somehow connected to the gold," DiNes mused, providing a reason for his questioning.

Without hesitation, Charles quickly responded, "It's highly doubtful, Sir. Your grandfather was a wealthy and shrewd businessman; he would have shown up long before the death of your mother to reclaim it. Your father, on the other hand, was too proud to ever think of taking anything, not to mention stealing from your grandfather. As I recall, there were fights about your father returning the dowry presented to him for your mother."

DiNes sat upright in his chair; it all made sense now. "So that's what I read in my father's journal. I couldn't quite make sense of it when I was reading. I guess my mind was focused on finding out more about this Priviot and D. Barclay. Grandfather was insulted and feared the state of my parents' matrimony. The refusal of the dowry could possibly mean a breach in the arrangement."

After DiNes spoke of his discovery, the two returned to their silent reverie, as if disturbed by what was said, sipping their scotch and leaving the topic for another occasion, should it need to be revisited. His mother had since passed on, and reopening a closed wound seemed unreasonable at the moment.

33

Chapter Eight

"All Hands on Deck"

The next morning, the mansion buzzed with a fresh sense of purpose. The air seemed crisper, the gardens more vibrant, as if the very estate sensed the renewed spirit of its inhabitants. In the heart of the bustling kitchen, Maria orchestrated a breakfast symphony that promised both comfort and nourishment for the long day ahead. Her skilled hands moved effortlessly across the countertop, bringing together ingredients with the harmony of a seasoned maestro.

DiNes and Charles sat at the breakfast table, poring over maps and travel itineraries. Each detail, from the shortest route to France to the most efficient way to find the Barclay shipping company, was being scrutinized and perfected. The tantalizing aroma of crepes filled the dining room, as Maria gracefully served the breakfast that promised to fuel their energy and spirits. The crepes were golden and filled with a medley of fresh fruits, accompanied by a side of fluffy scrambled eggs that were cooked to perfection. DiNes paused, taking a moment to appreciate the familial warmth that enveloped them. It had been a while since the mansion had echoed with deliberate voices and shared goals. He raised his coffee cup, signaling for a pause, "Before we dive into our plans, I just want to say thank you to both of you. You've stood by me through thick and thin, and as we embark on this journey, I want you to know that your support means the world to me."

Charles gave a nod, his eyes gleaming with loyalty and a touch of emotion. Maria, ever the stoic rock, simply squeezed DiNes's shoulder affectionately before returning to the kitchen. The moment lingered, a beautiful testament to the bond they shared, before they delved back into their planning, determined and united. They discussed strategies and contingencies, leaving no stone unturned in their quest to unravel the mysteries that seemed intertwined with the VàsSon legacy.

Hours later, as the sun began its descent, DiNes finally leaned back in his chair, a satisfied grin on his face. They had a solid plan in place, and soon they would set off to France, chasing clues and hopefully uncovering the secrets that lay hidden in the annals of history. As night fell, the trio congregated in the study once again, a makeshift war room where their strategies took shape. With maps spread out before them and notes scattered across the table, they vowed to unearth the truths that lay buried, not just for the sake of the VàsSon legacy, but for justice, for closure, and for the promise of a brighter, unburdened future.

As DiNes sat in his favorite chair, he thought of something ...the voice it seemed to have disappeared altogether, perhaps it would return. He couldn't be certain, however, the uneasy feeling he use to get just thinking about it seem to have dissipated. Perhaps Dr. Stoge was right maybe it was just his conscious invoking him to make changes in his life. DiNes decided that he would take it one day at a time and today the voice wasn't haunting him.

Maria broke the lingering silence. "How long might you chaps be away?"

DiNes considered the question thoughtfully, "It's hard to say. A week, perhaps two, depending on our findings."

Charles, ever the one to lighten the mood, cheekily remarked, "You're a resourceful lass, Maria. I wager you'll keep the house in tip-top shape in our absence."

Maria's laughter filled the room. "Oh, I dare say I'll relish the peace and quiet." Taking a measured sip of his brandy,

DiNes teased, "Now, Maria, surely you'll miss our incessant calls for meals, our endless laundry, and all the other delightful tasks we heap upon you." DiNes gave a wry smile, taking another sip. "Your dedication, in the face of our many demands, is most commendable." Lifting her glass in mock salute,

Maria rejoined with smirk, "Well, Mr. VàsSon, it's my purse that makes it all bearable."

Maria had always had a sharp instinct, a quality that served her well in maneuvering the delicate dynamics of the VàsSon household. DiNes's recent change in demeanor hadn't escaped her observant eyes. Charles tell me what's going on with DiNes, I know you two are planning to uncover this mystery but something is not quite right, and I see this, this sadness in his eyes. Confide in me won't you?" Maria beckoned.

Charles could not help himself he knew Maria had the best intentions for DiNes he was like her very own son. Charles told Maria everything including the debauched meeting he planned with Magdalena's father.

"Why didn't he come to me I know the head maid at her uncle's estate I could have arranged a meeting." Maria exclaimed.

"Well too late for that now I'm afraid the ship has sailed." Charles replied

For Maria it wasn't over and the news from Charles only stoked the fires of her curiosity and intrigue. She knew that love had a way of bringing about immense change, and DiNes was no exception. Throughout the week, Maria found herself humming as she went about her duties, a melodious tune that seemed to mirror the renewed energy in the mansion. The staff noticed the difference too, exchanging glances and smiles, uplifted by the infectious spirit of hope that seemed to permeate the house.

As the weekend approached, Maria anticipated her visit to the Pondeaux estate with a mix of excitement and resolve. She was determined to lend a helping hand in mending the strained relations between DiNes and Magdalena's family, especially considering the weighty matters that were at play. On the day of her visit, Maria dressed in her Sunday best, a neat ensemble that spoke of elegance and grace. The Pondeaux estate was not too far an hour's ride, nestled amidst lush greenery, a testament to the family's longstanding legacy. Maria was greeted by the head maid, Tudy Prejac, a woman of around her age, with a stern yet kind countenance.

After exchanging pleasantries and indulging in a cup of fine tea, Maria gently broached the topic at hand. "Tudy, you know the young master, DiNes VàsSon, don't you? I believe he has been acquainted with Miss Magdalena?" Maria queried, careful to tread lightly.

Tudy paused, her eyes narrowing slightly as she considered her words. "Aye, I know of him. Miss Magdalena has not made much mention of him, at least not frequently. There was some...unpleasantness involving Mr. Pondeaux, as I understand."

"Aye," Maria nodded her expression empathetic. "Yes, it was an unfortunate incident. But I must tell you, DiNes is genuinely repentant. He's been going through a significant change, and his feelings for Magdalena are sincere. I've never seen him so committed to making amends and building a new reputation." Tudy studied Maria, her gaze penetrating yet not unkind.

After a moment, she sighed, her stern facade softening. "I can see you care for him greatly, Maria. I trust your judgment. I will convey your sentiments to Magdalena when she is here next. Though, I cannot promise anything, it is ultimately her decision to make. I can tell you her father will be the greatest influence in the matter"

"Please, Tudy," Maria implored, her hands clasped tightly together, "I know Mr. Pondeaux has every reason to be wary, but DiNes is truly changing. He understands the gravity of his past mistakes and is willing to do whatever it takes to make amends. I've served the VàsSon family for many years, and I've never seen him like this before. His resolve, his determination to be better... it's quite remarkable."

Tudy sighed, her gaze drifting towards the window where the soft rays of the afternoon sun cast a warm glow on the lush gardens of the estate. "You know how protective Mr. Pondeaux is over Magdalena, Maria. Convincing him won't be easy, but I believe in second chances. People can change sometimes they just need the opportunity to prove it." Tudy offered Maria a comforting smile, reaching out to squeeze her hand reassuringly. "I will do my best, Maria. I'll speak with Magdalena first and gauge her feelings on the matter. If she is willing, I will try to bridge the conversation with Mr. Pondeaux. But remember, this road may be long and fraught with challenges."

Maria nodded, her eyes shimmering with tears that threatened to spill over. "Yes, and DiNes is no exception. He deserves a chance to show everyone the kind of man he is becoming."

"Magdalena has a gentle, forgiving heart. I just pray her father can find it within himself to extend the same grace." Trudy re-joined.

Maria smiled softly and nodded her heart swelling with gratitude. "Thank you, Tudy. That's all we can ask for. Now tell me how you have been getting along these days?"

"Why I've been just fine, the boys are all off on their own now, each married with a set of children of their own." Trudy replied.

"That's good to hear, you'll give everyone my best won't you?" Maria replied.

"Most certainly, as for you, have you and that Charles decided to get married and go off on your own? I don't mean to pry, but I know your heart dear and it has yearned for him for quite some time now. My eyes may be getting dim but I can still see the desire that burns within you." Trudy said as she fondly stroked Maria's hand.

"Oh hush with your foolish talk woman, one love at a time. I am here on the matter of your Magdalena and my DiNes." Maria managed to say while turning beak red and pulling her hand away.

Trudy lovingly grabbed Maria's hand back placed it on her lap and looked her firmly in the eyes and spoke "Aye no need to silence me, I know what I'm talking about the two of you never marrying or having children it's because you're both too stubborn to admit your love for one another.

Maria was out done, too out done to fight she simply hung her head down in embarrassment. "Well I suppose you do have a point Trudy, it's just the timing never seemed right. Me being a lady well I don't want to make the first move." Maria confessed.

"Aye I see your point, well Christmas is approaching, Daniel and I will just have to have you two over for a quiet Christmas celebration." Trudy replied with a devilish grin. The two laughed and continued with light conversation. After a while Maria announced her departure. The two hugged and bid each other Farwell. As Maria stepped out into the cool late afternoon, a renewed sense of hope filled her. The path to redemption and love was not easy, but perhaps, with time and patience, DiNes and Magdalena could find their proper way into each other's hearts, building bridges where once there were only chasms as for she and Charles that was another story that would have to wait.

Chapter Nine

"An Opportunity for Love"

During Magdalena's subsequent visit, Trudy held true to her word. She approached Magdalena with the suggestion of forgiving DiNes and considering his advances.

"Trudy, you've always been someone I could rely on to respect my confidence," Magdalena responded, her voice tinged with hesitation. "I won't deny that I find him fascinating. Yet, his notoriety seems to eclipse this newfound demeanor you speak of. And even if I could look past that, I fear my father and uncle might not, they are potentially standing against any alliance between us."

With an unwavering glint in her eye, Trudy retorted, "I could always have a word with your uncle; I've managed to persuade him in the past. But first, I need to know if pursuing this is genuinely what you desire." Her tone was stern, urging Magdalena to introspect deeply.

Magdalena sighed, a flicker of confusion and curiosity dancing in her eyes. "The truth is, Trudy, I barely know him. We shared a brief, yet magnetic, exchange by the shore. I was undeniably captivated, finding myself drawn towards him time and again in my thoughts, even going so far as to inquire about him discreetly. But his tarnished reputation has halted any progression in our acquaintance. Despite this, I can't shake this budding affinity, this intrigue I hold for him. I find myself at a crossroads, unsure of which path to tread."

Trudy nodded, her expression softening. "In that case, before I advocate for you to your uncle, it will be wise to give yourself the space to decipher your true feelings, to understand where your heart truly lies."

Magdalena, feeling the burden of the swirling rumors and the weight of the choices before her, sought solace in the tranquil company of her cousin Lisette however, fondly referred to as Lissy. Underneath a grand oak, bathed in dapples of sunlight, they found themselves deep in conversation. Lisette, a fountain of wisdom and warmth, listened intently as Magdalena poured out her hesitations. Magdalena, her voice tinged with a hint of vulnerability, said, "I find myself at crossroads, Lissy. I wish to honor my father's wishes and respect his insights, but I also can't ignore the spark DiNes ignited within me. Lissy you live on this island, you know torrid details of his disreputable past, what are your thoughts on the two of us?"

Lisette took a moment before responding, her eyes reflecting the deep empathy she felt for her cousin. "Magdalena, love is a risk, a gamble where you wager your heart hoping to find happiness and companionship. But you're not a naive girl anymore. You've known love and loss. You've shouldered responsibilities beyond your years. It's high time you considered your happiness too. However on the other hand DiNes has quite the reputation," Lissy leaned forward, her voice low and urgent. "Magdalena, I've heard the whispers about DiNes too, his affairs, his trysts with Amoremea, all while she's allegedly in some commitment to Pierre Dubois. Town gossips have certainly had their fill with these tales. But you must remember, these are just rumors, flimsy and fleeting."

Magdalena's gaze dropped to her hands, folded tensely in her lap. "But what if there's truth in them, Lissy? They say he's a master of deception. That beneath his charm, there's a world of secrets. I can't help but fear that I'm walking into a storm."

Lissy reached out, gently squeezing Magdalena's hand. "Then confront the storm, Maggie. Speak with DiNes. Let him tell his side of the story, let him unveil whatever truth he holds. Make your judgment based on that, not on idle talk."

Magdalena took a deep breath, nodding slowly. "You're right, Lissy. I need to hear it from him, face to face. I deserve that clarity, and perhaps, so does he." You can see it in my eyes, can't you, Lissy?" A blend of hope and fear swirling endlessly," Magdalena said with a vulnerability that tugged at Lissy's heart. "You're absolutely right, I owe it to both myself and to him to unearth the truth, to forge a road grounded in genuine feelings and insights, not guided by the deceit woven by others."

Lissy nodded emphatically, giving Magdalena's hand a comforting squeeze. "Magdalena, you must follow your heart, but do it with your eyes wide open, seeking truth and joy wherever it might be hiding," she urged her.

With a somber tone, Magdalena continued, "Well, cousin, for the moment, I intend to remain in solitude. Trudy, your headmistress, revealed his plans to me. I'm in the dark about whether my father and uncle will accept our courtship. I don't know if I should send an invitation to him to greet me here at your home. I think it's too soon to decide, uncle and father still have that night circling in the forefront of their thoughts. I'd like to have a little more time to mull things over and consult with my father when the time is right."

Lissy nodded, her face a canvas of understanding and concern. "In this scenario, you must communicate with Trudy," she advised. "She needs to convey your current sentiments to your suitor to avoid an untimely visit here."

"I will do so just before father and I depart." Magdalena replied.

"Magdalena, you haven't uttered a word since we left, the ferry journey was quite solitary, wasn't it?" Mr. Pondeaux initiated his face a map of worry. "Maggie, are you certain you're alright?" Usually, you're brimming with stories and chatter during our rides," he pressed, his hands on her shoulder and moved gently up to her cheek, trying to feel for any signs of distress.

Magdalena offered a comforting squeeze on her father's hand. "No need to worry, Father. It's just that Lissy and I had quite a profound conversation earlier. I need some time to reflect on it, that's all. I'm sorry if I'm keeping to myself a bit too much tonight," she assured him, her voice holding a quiet strength.

Mr. Pondeaux, however, couldn't shake off the knot of concern tightening in his stomach. The memories of her recent widowhood and the unsavory encounter with Mr. VàsSon made him apprehensive about her well-being. "But you're certain you're sharing everything with me, aren't you?" he probed, a hint of concern weaving through his words.

"Absolutely, Father," Magdalena responded, punctuating her assurance with a soft kiss on his cheek. She could feel her father's suspicious gaze lingering, especially regarding her interactions with DiNes. If only DiNes hadn't forced that initial introduction, tarnishing his own reputation slightly and solidifying rumors. "I need to be tactful about introducing the possibility of a courtship between us," Magdalena mused silently. "If only mother were here, she might have been able to soften father's stance." She felt a pang of sadness thinking about her mother - a figure who had ironically contributed to her father's existing mistrusts. Magdalena leaned against her father, her head finding a comforting spot on his shoulder. "*I wish mother could have helped in this situation,*" she whispered in her mind, her thoughts drifting to the last encounter she shared with her mother and siblings....

The grand room of Magdalena's mother's new estate was filled with the faint stench of the haunt laughter, painful memories, and heartbreak her mother portrayed without remorse. The room, decorated with rich tapestries and portraits, were a facade to cover up the scandal and shame her mother bought on the family name. It was here that Magdalena decided to gather her family, hoping to find resolve in the parting of her parents. Magdalena's mother, Lady Isabella, elegantly dressed but with age reflecting in her eyes, sat poised yet distant. Her two sisters, Clarissa and Seraphina, always the more boisterous ones, whispered amongst themselves. Lissy, ever the comforting presence, sat close to Magdalena.

Breaking the silence, Magdalena asked, "Mother, why did you leave father when he needed you the most? I've never understood." Father continues to struggle with your absence. If he had his sight things might not be so hard but he is in the dark in more ways than one. I as well of the rest of my siblings have had to painfully watch him fight to keep his dignity, not just among his peers but society." Magdalena bravely said, as her words led to a flurry of tears streaming down her cheeks.

Lady Isabella took a moment, the weight of the past heavy in her voice, "Magdalena, love sometimes isn't enough. The pain of seeing your father, the man I once danced with under the stars, helpless... it broke me. I couldn't bear it."

Clarissa, always one to speak her mind, chimed in, "You felt father's misfortune threatened your position. Luxury and comfort is all you ever cared about not family, mother. Let's not romanticize your departure. If Father's misfortune wasn't enough to fold your heart and compel you to stay, I don't know what would"

Seraphina, a bit more understanding, added, "Clarissa, it wasn't easy for any of us. Let's not judge. We all made our choices."

Lissy, trying to mediate, said, "Family is complicated. Everyone carries their burdens, their regrets. What's important is how we move forward."

Magdalena, tears flowing steady, whispered, "I've been the one holding everything together. While Clarissa and Seraphina went on to live their lives, I stayed. I cared for father, our home."

Seraphina, feeling guilty, admitted, "You've always been the strong one, Maggie. We took that for granted."

Clarissa added, "I always admired your resilience. I just wish we had been there for you."

Magdalena sighed, "What stopped you? All I've ever wanted was for us to be a family and face our trials together. I too suffered a loss but it did not keep me from being at father's side when he needed us the most. I made my peace with Lucas's death and resumed my duties as an honorable daughter."

Lady Isabella, voice trembling, said, "It's never too late, my dear. We're here now. Let's mend what's broken, as for me and your father I doubt we will reunite. As I can see he has learned to get along just fine without me. He has redeemed his reputation among his peers and his fortune is still intact. Believe it or not I am grateful for that."

The room was thick with emotion as the Pondeaux family grappled with raw confessions, searching for a glimmer of hope amidst their fractured history. They were hoping for new beginnings, relying on each other for strength and a brighter future. Yet, as Isabelle's confessional words hung in the air, the room's heavy atmosphere was interrupted by the sudden appearance of her new husband.

"Why such somber faces? Is this a gathering or a funeral?" Franz jested as he entered the room, sweeping Isabelle into his arms and twirling her around, her melodic laughter filling the space.

The siblings exchanged glances, the weight of the moment now seemingly lightened by their mother's jovial disposition. "A leopard never changes its spots," Seraphina remarked, raising her champagne flute in a half-toast. As she took a sip, Lissy squeezed Magdalena's hand, a silent acknowledgment that, despite their best efforts, the hoped-for family reconciliation seemed once again just out of reach.

"God I hope I am never like her." Magdalena whispered to Lissy.

Magdalena lay enveloped in memories, reliving that day. The fear of turning into a mirror image of her mother gnawed at her. Could DiNes be the one to draw out that side of her? Maybe she should write to Trudy, revisiting her previous decision. She nestled closer to her father, longing for the days of innocence when she was unaware of the world's wickedness and relied solely on her father to console her after every misadventure. Yet, the truth remained - she was a grown woman of thirty-three, her initiation into the fullness of womanhood, love, and marriage halted abruptly by Lucas's death. The deep yearning to carry a life within her grew stronger with each passing day.

"Maggie," Sohan began, sensing her desolation, "how about we take a trip to the Foire aux Plaisirs on Saturday? We could indulge in some des frites with dipping sauce, ice cream, and of course, your favorite chocolate!" He desperately wanted to pull her out of the depths of her contemplation, sensing an undercurrent of sorrow that wasn't there before. Over a year had passed since Lucas's death, and though Maggie strived to stay positive, Sohan feared she was losing ground. He had even considered offering her tranquilizers but was wary of the potential dependency. He knew the road ahead was tough, but he was determined to show Maggie that there was, indeed, life after Lucas.

"Yes father that would be nice." Magdalena replied in a distant dry tone. Perhaps a day at the fair would be a nice retreat it just might be the antidote she'd been looking for. Chocolate was her favorite after all, in fact too hard to resist, besides father could use some refreshing as well.

For now Magdalena would leave the matter of courtship between her and DiNes alone. She would focus on letting go of Lucas, before embarking on a new love. No one not even DiNes deserved to live in the shadow of a ghost. This small adventure with her father to Paris on Saturday would be full of excitement and adventure and she was looking forward to it. "Thanks father," Magdalena said as she lifted her head to his cheek and planted a firm kiss on it. "You are my hero you always know just want to do to bring me around don't you."

"Why thank you Maggie and you too are my heroine, you charm the monotony right out of me," Sohan replied feeling well accomplished.

Chapter 10

"The Journey Begins"

Charles and DiNes stood on the deck of the ferry, feeling the sea spray against their faces as they looked towards the distant French coast. "I've always like visiting France," Charles remarked, adjusting his coat against the sea breeze. "Though I never thought it would be under such mysterious circumstances."

DiNes chuckled, "Yes, this gold is truly taking us on an adventure. First stop is Mr. Priviot's valet Don Marc."

Charles, squinting into the horizon said, "I've heard a lot about Cannes. Never been though, they say it's a jewel of the Riviera."

DiNes nodded. "My main concern is finding Don DaMarc, Mr. Priviot's valet. I hope he can provide us some answers."

As the ferry docked, and they anticipated their journey through the bustling streets of Cannes, Charles turned to DiNes. "So, we are meeting our first contact, Mr. Marc. Think he will be welcoming?"

The ferry anchored at La Croisette. The two entered their car and drove alongside the boulevard, savoring the beauty of the Mediterranean Sea. Following the map, they embarked on their journey through the Old Quarters of Cannes. Driving with the windows down, they were greeted by the savory aromas wafting from Forville Market. Among the main sites to see was the Musée de la Castre. Finally, they arrived in Le Suquet, offering the most stunning view of all, showcasing the entire port of the city. Down Rue Saint Antoine lay Don DaMarc's estate. Le Suquet, with its cobblestone roads, epitomized the historical charm of Cannes.

"So much for a smooth ride, aye Charles?" DiNes joked as the two bounced up and down during the ride.

"No, Sir. I'm afraid not, but the view is marvelous—positively medieval," Charles chuckled. He wondered if they'd have time to visit the 15th-century Église Notre-Dame d'Espérance church.

"We're about to find out," DiNes replied, approaching the grandeur of Mr. DaMarc's estate. Upon entering, they were greeted by an elderly, well-dressed man.

"Good day Monsieur I am DiNes VàsSon and this is my assistant Charles LaMôur. DiNes said as he extended his hand to Don.

"Ah, Monsieur DiNes and Monsieur Charles I am Don DaMarc at your service. Welcome to Cannes. What can I do for you?" Don replied shaking DiNes's and Charles's hand.

"Thank you for meeting us, Mr. DaMarc. We've traveled from the Ile Saint Marguerite, chasing a mystery involving my father and Mr. Priviot," DiNes started, trying to gauge the man's reaction. DaMarc nodded, gesturing them inside. Once inside DiNes begin explaining his situation without divulging news of the gold he and Charles discovered. He just simply stated that he had stumbled across something of importance in his father's old journals and believed there were missing details that not only involved his father, but the Priviot and Barclays.

"Yes, I am aware of their relationship. The Barclay family shipping company and your father's designs, quite a legacy you should be proud. Come, let's discuss this further." After a brief but enlightening conversation with Don, DiNes and Charles learned that Don didn't have enough information to fill the gaps of the mystery, but gave them a clue Manotè,

Mr. Priviot's grandson who lives in Monte Carlo, Monaco. Charles and DiNes collected the address, thanked Don for all of his help and left for left for Monaco.

The drive to Monaco was far more scenic, offering them breathtaking views of the Mediterranean. Monaco, being a very small country with only one city, provided a unique charm. As DiNes and Charles drove in, they marveled at the sight of the Prince's Palace of Monaco, a structure built in the 13th century and an extraordinary landmark. The Vass Cove of Port de la Condamine added to the picturesque setting. Monotè's residence was located near Blvd des Moulins, MC, a bustling yet ritzy area not far from the Sainte-Devote Chapel.

Upon arrival, they were welcomed warmly by Manotè Priviot, the grandson of Mr. Priviot. They were invited to partake in a lavish dinner.

"Ah, DiNes! Charles! It's a pleasure," Manotè greeted, his smile wide. "I was just about to sit down for dinner. Would you two like to join me? I've heard much about your father's craftsmanship."

"That's good to know. Perhaps you will be able to answer some questions for us," DiNes said, following Manotè toward the dining hall. Upon arrival, Manotè instructed the maid to set two more places at the table.

"Gentlemen, I'd like to introduce you to my wife, Antoinette, and these are my two children, Elisabeth and Henry," Manotè said as his wife and two small children entered the dining hall. After everyone was seated, a glass of red wine was poured for each guest, and dinner was served. As the meal progressed, DiNes and Charles began filling Manotè in on their inquiries.

DiNes, slicing into a tender piece of meat, inquired, "We've come to understand more about the business your grandfather had with my father, one ship in particular that carried some very valuable cargo."

Manotè leaned back, swirling his wine, "I believe my father Paul can shed more light on this as it was somewhat before my time. But first, eat, rest and tomorrow, I'll send you to him."

DiNes and Charles did eat and enjoy the company. The children were wildly entertaining while Antoinette did his best to contain them. Manotè apologized profusely for their rambunctious behavior. At the end of their meal they were shown the guest quarters, Charles and DiNes settled in and got plenty of rest for the day ahead.

Revelations at Marseille

The journey to Marseille had become increasingly challenging, thanks to the unrelenting weather. An hour and fifteen minutes into their drive, a dense grey canopy had formed in the sky, releasing a torrential downpour. Charles, at the wheel, strained to see through the windshield despite the wipers' best efforts. Determinedly, they continued for another half-hour before finally reaching Marseille.

Exhaustion was evident on their faces. "I say, DiNes, we ought to find shelter for the night. This weather shows no signs of abating," Charles exclaimed, raising his voice to combat the drumming rain. DiNes, spotting The Grand Hotel Beauvau Marseille Vieux-Port-MGallery, responded with fatigue evident in his voice, "I suggest we stay here for the evening." "Agreed!" Charles concurred with relief.

That evening, the two settled into the warmth of the Grand Hotel Beauvau Marseille's restaurant. The hotel's enviable position in Phocean City meant it was nestled right at the foot of La Cannebière and only a short 10-minute stroll from the renowned Palais du Pharo. The allure of Marseille was undeniable, with its sprawling coves and the historic Château d'If. Moreover, the Docks added a unique flavor to the city's rich tapestry. As the evening progressed, a lively chat with the bartender connected them to a knowledgeable local. This older man, radiating a welcoming aura, regaled them with tales of the region's aristocrats. So taken were they by the ambiance and the stories that they chose to spend the night at the hotel, eager to dive back into business the next morning.

It was business as usual in Marseille bright and early the next morning, where they were met by Paul Priviot, who welcomed them warmly. Paul, with a nostalgic smile, started, "Ah, DiNes, your father and mine, they were quite the businessmen. I can tell you man tales my father shared with me."

Over a hearty meal, DiNes explained to Paul he and Charles's latest discover. DiNes showed Paul the note he found in his father journal along with a few of the logs he found in the chest and notes he found in his father's journal pertaining to the lost cargo. Paul relayed what he knew of the enigmatic tale of the gold shipment and the storm that claimed the vessel. How his father had employed Mr. Barclay to facilitate the transportation, which had then turned into a nightmare as the ship was lost to the tempestuous sea.

"I must tell you, my father was a secretive man. Before he could tell me the entire story, death claimed him. But I believe, it is time to find out the truth behind the missing gold and the ship. I believe your father's role in this was he designed the fleet," Paul said, a flicker of sadness in his eyes.

DiNes listened with a heavy heart, absorbing the gravity of their mission. "Your next step should be meeting Hugo Barclay. He resides in Saint Pierre (Saint Peter) Port, Guernsey. He might hold the key to solving this," Paul suggested, handing over an address.

Charles leaned in, "This journey is turning out to be much bigger than we anticipated, isn't it DiNes?"

DiNes nodded solemnly, the weight of their quest settling on his shoulders, "Yes, it is. But we must uncover the truth, not just for us, but for the ones who were lost to the sea."

With new information and an advantageous determination, they bid farewell to Paul, ready to venture to Guernsey, and possibly, the final chapter of their unfolding mystery. It was an 18 hour trip to Saint Pierre (Peter) Port, Guernsey. Charles and DiNes would drive 6 hours to Bordeaux and rest. The following day they plan to drive 12 hours to Saint-Malo Porte de Dinan and boarded the ferry to Saint Pierre (Peter) Port Guernsey.

Actionable Intel at Bordeaux

Charles and DiNes could not resist the opportunity to venture to a traditional restaurant while in Marseille the recommendations from Paul made them curious and allure was undeniable with the coves and the historic Château d'If right at their fingertips DiNes and Charles were not going to pass up the opportunity. Moreover, the Docks wreaked for fresh smells of baking bread, and the tantalizing aroma of coffee.

Having concluded their lunch by 1:30 p.m., the duo prepared to embark on their journey. Charles perused the map just before starting the car. "DiNes, if we follow this route, we should make it to Bordeaux right in time for dinner," he remarked.

"Sounds like a plan. You drive the first three hours, and I'll take over from there," DiNes proposed.

"Perfect," agreed Charles, and they set off. The journey took them to Montalba, where they paused briefly to refuel. Then, DiNes assumed the driving duties. As they approached Bordeaux, the renowned Le Chapon Fin Depuis restaurant caught Charles' eye.

DiNes, his stomach audibly rumbling, asked, "Hungry, Charles?" Charles chuckled in response,

"You've read my mind, Sir. I'm absolutely famished!" Without a moment's delay, DiNes parked the car, and the two eagerly entered the restaurant, anticipating a sumptuous meal.

The Maître D' guided DiNes and Charles to a table adjacent to four gentlemen, who were deeply engrossed in convivial conversation. As they savored dessert, the allure of Cognac shimmered in their fine crystal wobble snifters. The rich aroma of the Cognac captivated DiNes, and he found himself subtly eavesdropping on their discussion. Meanwhile, Charles, engrossed in the map and periodically sipping his French wine, remained oblivious to the neighboring chatter. The wine in Bordeaux is very famous for its award winning vineyard scattered about in the city.

DiNes discreetly eavesdropped on a conversation between two gentlemen nearby. Their words piqued his interest when the name Lucas emerged, a young man who tragically passed away at the age of thirty-four. But when mentions of Magdalena and her father, Sohan Pondeaux, were woven into the narrative, DiNes was sure of the connection. "Could they be discussing the Pondeaux family?" he mused, finding it strangely coincidental how often he stumbled upon conversations about the Pondeaux lineage in local cafés and taverns. As the talk continued, it became evident that one of the conversationalists was Lucas's uncle. The man's tone grew somber as he expressed his sympathies for Magdalena, lamenting the change in her demeanor since the tragic event. Seizing this opportunity, DiNes began contemplating a subtle approach to glean more details, especially the man's address, without revealing too much of his own interest.

"I say, comrades, pardon my impertinence, but I believe I heard the two of you discussing a man in whom I am quite interested. A Mr. Sohan Pondeaux, I presume?" DiNes interjected. The men were startled by DiNes's interruption and were somewhat apprehensive about replying.

"Why, yes, we were. And who might you be?" one of the men exclaimed.

"I—well, I am Mr. DiNes VàsSon, at your service," DiNes said, extending his hand towards the men. "I couldn't help but overhear your conversation. Mr. Pondeaux is well-known where I come from; we really admire his work. I'm visiting France on other important matters but would appreciate the opportunity to pop in and pay my respects to he and his daughter, I hadn't had the opportunity to express my condolences for the young Mr. Lucas," DiNes continued, explaining his intentions. The men were soon put at ease by DiNes's reply and provided him with Mr. Pondeaux's address.

"Their estate is just a little way up in Bordeaux, not too far from here." Lucas's uncle wrote down the address and handed it to DiNes.

DiNes and Charles shared a brief, meaningful glance. With a hint of resolve, DiNes took a deliberate sip from his glass, placing it back on the table with a look of determination. "Gentlemen," he began, "thank you for the directions. And please, excuse our interruption. Might you also know of a suitable lodging nearby for the night?"

One of the men promptly suggested, "D'hôtel Particular Bordeaux would be an excellent choice." Charles, keen on the idea, inquired,

"And how far might that be from here?" "Just a four-minute drive," the gentleman responded. "Simply follow Rue du Dr. Charles Nancel Penard. It's quite straightforward." DiNes and Charles thanked the Bordelais and prepared to make their way to the D'hôtel Particular Bordeaux.

"Charles, I think we need to make a quick detour."

"DiNes, I don't think that is wise. This weather doesn't seem to be in our favor, and I would hate to get stuck without finishing our primary business. Let us not get distracted; we can complete our business first and make the detour on the way back," Charles reasoned.

"Very well, Charles. Thank God for your practicality—where would I be without you?" DiNes rejoined with a heartfelt sigh.

"Well, sir, that's what I'm here for," Charles replied with a warm smile.

"The Curse of the Gold"

As the ferry approached Guernsey, DiNes felt a palpable rush of excitement. The enigma that had consumed his thoughts was now gradually unveiling itself. Beside him, Charles, though wearied from the voyage, mirrored DiNes' sense of purpose. Their seven-hour journey to Saint Peter Port had been taxing, but their spirit remained undeterred. The journey treated them to breathtaking views of Bordeaux, showcasing vast architecture that proudly displayed the city's rich cultural heritage. Among the most astounding sights was the "Pearl of Aquitaine." Fueled by determination, they pressed on, arriving at Hugo Barclay's mansion just as the evening's chilled embrace began to settle in.

They were met with a stark contrast from their earlier encounters; Hugo exuded a melancholic demeanor, an aura of years weighted with unresolved grief and bitterness. However, he led them to the well-lit patio, a somewhat comforting ambiance amidst the looming darkness of the evening.

As the butler attended to Hugo's requests, DiNes began hesitantly, "Mr. Barclay, we are here to uncover the truth, about our recent findings. It seems my father had been retaining something a value... something that may have belonged to your father and Mr. Priviot..."

"Yes gentlemen I know all about it, I suppose you're here for an explanation?" Hugo replied reaching for the half empty pack of cigarettes lying on the table next to an ashtray filled with ashes and cigarette butts.

Hugo lit a cigarette, the orange glow casting eerie shadows on his solemn face. "I don't expect anything good to come from dredging up the past, DiNes. But for your sake I will tell you the story of a lost ship at sea and it's tainted cargo, this is the account of events that my father passed on to me." With the smoke swirling around them, DiNes and Charles listened intently, as Hugo began his tale. The night air was thick with the scent of whiskey and the bitterness of past regrets.

"My brothers were just boys, barely adolescents, when they concocted a perilous prank to stow away on my uncle's ship - the very vessel under my uncle's command. Driven by the adventurous tales overheard from my father and Mr. Priviot discussing the gold transport, they envisioned it as a chance for a rumbustious adventure, a real-life pirate escapade. At that tender age, they couldn't possibly fathom the grave consequences of their impromptu decision.

They concealed themselves behind the hefty trunk harboring the gold when the tempest struck, an unforeseen force that treated them with no mercy. The relentless tides and vicious winds flung them mercilessly against the trunk..." Here, Hugo paused, a visible struggle to maintain his composure evident on his face.

"The ship was battered unceasingly, tossed to and fro in the raging storm. In the chaos, the ropes binding the trunk frayed and finally gave way, releasing the trunk with a force unhindered. It slammed into my brothers, pinning them against the ship's wall where splintered wood protruded, a result of the relentless battering from the rampant cargo."

Charles murmured sympathetically, "That's a horrendous way for a young life to end..."

Hugo nodded, sipping his whiskey before continuing, "My uncle was heartbroken when he found them, battered and barely hanging onto life. They managed to survive until they reached the shore, but the island offered no solace, no medical aid..."

'DiNes could feel his heart growing heavy, a manifestation of the shared grief connecting them to their ancestors in that moment. Hugo, with evident raw pain in his voice continued, 'They perished on that forsaken island, leaving my uncle burdened by their loss. Neither Mr. Priviot nor my father desired any connection to the gold; they perceived it as cursed, a token marking the tragedy that befell our family. The origins of Mr. Priviot's acquisition of the gold remain undisclosed; I don't believe it holds any significance at this point.

"The air grew denser as the moon climbed higher. Hugo's face was bathed in moonlight, his eyes glistening with tears held back for too long. DiNes took a deep breath, unveiling his own revelations, "Hugo, I found the gold... In a cave adjacent to my family's home in Ile Sainte Marguerite. I am here to offer you and Paul your shares, as rightful heirs."

Hugo shook his head vehemently, "No, DiNes. That gold... it robbed me of a father's love, a childhood filled with joy. My father grieved my brothers for all of my childhood. Neither I nor my sisters were ever able to capture my father's affection. I want nothing to do with it."

DiNes reached over giving Hugo a firm pat on the back, "I understand, Hugo. This journey has brought much-needed closure, an understanding of our fathers' actions, and perhaps a chance to heal." As the night wore on, they shared more stories, more whiskey, and more empathy. It was a night of healing, of three men bound by the past, seeking solace and closure in the moonlit garden. "Surely you must not punish yourself any longer, allow me to compensate you with what is rightfully yours." DiNes pleaded.

Hugo extracted yet another cigarette from his nearly depleted pack, igniting it and inhaling deeply, seemingly immersed in profound contemplation. He exhaled slowly, the smoke hanging momentarily in the air before dissipating. But as the ember of the cigarette flickered, Hugo seemed to gather himself. His shoulders squared, his eyes regained their sparkle, reflecting the fiery sky. Hugo finally broke his silence, his voice gravelly yet soft, carrying a weight of experience and depth.

'No, old boy, I believe me and my family are better off without that cursed gold. Besides, the gold never truly belonged to my father; it was Mr. Priviot's property. My father was merely the transporter, and he was more than compensated for his troubles. Your father was a part of the search crew that repaired the ship and sailed it back to God knows where. It seems that wherever he sailed to, he stumbled upon the gold. He showed great honor by informing my father and Mr. Priviot of his discovery. As I was told, there was a discussion regarding what should be done with the gold, but neither my father nor Mr. Priviot ever sought to reclaim it. From what I understand, the insurance company reimbursed Mr. Priviot for his losses. I hate to say it, but your journey may have been in vain if you were seeking redemption by returning this gold.'

"Very well then, I guess Charles and I will be on our way, we won't keep you any longer." DiNes said as he and Charles stood up from the table.

"I am not sure where you two have chosen to lodge this evening but you are more than welcome to lodge here at my estate we have plenty of room and would be most happy to accommodate you." Hugo said looking up at the two of them.

DiNes looked at Charles as though he was seeking his approval. "Whatever you decided is quite alright with me" Charles replied.

"Well if it's not too much trouble, we would like to take you up on the offer." DiNes responded.

"Yes of course, by the way, your father designed our entire fleet, if there is time perhaps you would like to take a gander at them before your go." Hugo said as he smashed his cigarette in the ash tray.

The next morning, DiNes and Charles followed Hugo's suggestion, driving to the Port to witness the legacy of DiNes's late father, Winston. There it was—an impressive fleet of ships, some gracefully sailing at sea. As DiNes observed the meticulous craftsmanship of the vessels, he felt his heart soften. He couldn't help but appreciate the intelligence and skill that must have defined his father's work, and his respect for him began to resurface.

Charles and DiNes expanded their exploration by visiting Castle Cornet, a fortress that had guarded the harbor for over 800 years. The panoramic view from the Castle left them in awe. Their journey continued to the Guernsey Tapestry, where they immersed themselves in the rich culture depicted on canvases spanning over a thousand years. Each artwork represented centuries of profound history.

Before their return to Bordeaux, they made a final stop at the House of Victor Hugo. The house showcased Hugo's exceptional artistic talent and discerning taste, while the garden offered a breathtaking display of the lush and rare botanicals unique to Guernsey.

Chapter Eleven

"Resolutions and Revelations"

With the sun painting the sky in soft hues of orange, DiNes and Charles commenced their journey home. DiNes was contemplative, the heavy weight of the stories and revelations from the previous night still echoing in his mind. During lunch in a quaint café, DiNes could feel Charles' watchful eyes on him, sensing the turmoil within his friend.

Charles finally broke the silence, his voice carrying a note of concern, "You've been quiet, DiNes. What's going through your mind?"

DiNes looked up, his eyes reflecting the turmoil of his soul. "Charles, I can't shake the feeling that perhaps that gold has tainted not just the Barclay family but mine as well. My own upbringing wasn't without its shadows."

Charles leaned back, his expression thoughtful. "DiNes, sometimes circumstances and choices shape us more than curses do. We cannot let the past dictate our futures."

DiNes nodded, seemingly in agreement. But as they continued their journey, a vivid memory struck him—a conversation he had once overheard between his father and Charles. They shared laughter, stories, and a bond that seemed unaffected by the tragedies of their lineage. DiNes suddenly realized that perhaps, individuals wield more power over their destinies than any perceived curse.

His face lit up with newfound resolution. "Charles, we are making two stops on our way back. The first is in Bordeaux. I intend to meet Mr. Pondeaux and settle things once and for all."

Charles raised his eyebrows in surprise but nodded in agreement. "And the second?"

DiNes smiled, the sun now fully bathing his face in a warm glow, symbolizing the dawning of a new chapter in his life. "We're visiting Paul again. I've realized that we have the power to define our own paths. It's time to bring some positivity back into our families, starting with sharing the fortune."

The journey felt lighter, the roads less daunting as Charles and DiNes made their way towards Bordeaux. Driving along the Port of the Moon, DiNes felt his heartbeat quicken. Meanwhile, Charles was captivated by the view, so much so that he entertained the idea of pulling the car over to fully immerse himself in the cool, fresh sea air rising from the port. Instead, he rolled down the car window, inhaling and exhaling slowly, savoring the beauty of the crescent path before them.

Upon arriving at the Pondeaux estate, DiNes felt a blend of anticipation and nervousness. DiNes and Charles approached the grandeur of the Pondeaux estate under the afternoon's sun that painted everything with a brush of hope. DiNes' hands were clammy, his stomach a bundle of nerves knotted tightly. Charles offered a reassuring squeeze on his shoulder. "Keep your composure, no matter what unfolds, allow me to do the talking" he reminded gently.

With a nod, DiNes steadied himself. The door was answered by a stoic doorman who seemed to survey them with piercing scrutiny before announcing, "Charles and his assistant are here to see you, Mr. Pondeaux." Led into the lavish drawing room, they found Mr. Pondeaux seated comfortably, his sightless eyes, a deep well of wisdom and experiences, turned towards the wall. The air thickened with tension as Charles cleared his throat to speak.

"Good afternoon, Mr. Pondeaux. My name is Charles LaMòur, I am here with my assistant," he began, his voice laced with a respectful firmness. "We are here to discuss a matter that is of significant importance." Mr. Pondeaux turned his head slightly in the direction of the voice, his face an unreadable mask as he processed the words. Yes, yes please come in and have a seat, "What can I do for you?!" Mr. Pondeaux asked intently

There was a pregnant pause. Charles wasn't quite sure how to begin. "Well Sir, you see Sir, this matter is very delicate it involves your daughter and"... Charles stopped mid-sentence.

"My daughter, please Sir go on, what matter of business do you have with my daughter? And by the way which daughter I have three." Mr. Pondeaux sharply replied.

"Ah yes well I am referring to Ms. Magdalena?" Charles replied.

"Magdalena! What on earth do you want with her?" Mr. Pondeaux exclaimed.

"Oh no, you needn't alarm yourself; I apologize if I alarmed you." Charles quickly intervened.

"Well out with it, you've piqued my curiosity in the most annoying way." Mr. Pondeaux retorted.

Charles held his ground. "Mr. Pondeaux, I beseech you, please lower your defenses as I tell you of a tail, a love story if you please between two pitiful souls, and a man who found that his affinity for her places him in the most peculiar predicament. You see my DiNes has fallen hopelessly in love with your Magdalena. He has accompanied me here today to confess his love for her in hopes to be requited." Charles implored.

"Oh ha I knew something was shifty from the moment you stepped in my residence out with the both of you, out!" Mr. Pondeaux bellowed.

"Mr. Pondeaux please I pray you would give us a chance to explain. DiNes has something to say, something - deeply connected to Magdalena."

A heavy silence settled, Mr. Pondeaux took a deep sigh. "This is truly against my better judgement. I have a bad feeling about this." Mr. Pondeaux took a few minutes more to ponder. Finally his silence was broken before Mr. Pondeaux signaled for them to continue.

DiNes, with his heart lodged firmly in his throat, began speaking, his voice trembling yet determined. "Mr. Pondeaux, I stand before you not as a harbinger of deceit, but as a man who wishes to mend his ways and evolve into someone deserving of respect." He paused, taking a breath as he gathered the fortitude to continue. "I have stumbled and faltered in life, yet meeting Magdalena has become a beacon of light, guiding me toward a path of redemption. I love her, sir, with an intensity that has bestowed upon me a renewed purpose and a desire to be a better man, both for her and for myself. If today you could find it in your heart to not only forgive me but also grant my request to pursue a relationship with your daughter, I vow to devote my entire existence to making Magdalena the happiest woman on this earth. Her heart would never know sorrow, and the only tears she would shed would be those of boundless joy. Together, the legacy of the Pondeaux and VàsSon families would flourish in the most loving and prodigious way."

"Though I'd prefer to dismiss you outright, the ultimate decision isn't mine to make alone. Just yesterday, Magdalena mentioned a potential courtship between you two, which I must admit, infuriated me. The very notion that she might entertain a liaison with someone of your reputed disposition seemed preposterous. I urged her to rethink, holding onto the hope that she would see reason. However, it appears that both of you are entangled in this bizarre affection for one another. It is only right to involve her in this discussion since her future is at stake here."

Mr. Pondeaux reached for a petite bell on the adjacent table and rang it, summoning the butler. The man entered promptly, standing at attention. "How may I assist you, Sir?" he greeted respectfully.

"Summon Magdalena, please. She should be part of this conversation," Mr. Pondeaux instructed, his voice carrying an undertone of seriousness.

"Right away, Sir," the butler responded, making a swift exit to carry out the command. Upon entering the room,

Magdalena was struck with surprise at the sight of DiNes and Charles, given that she hadn't revealed her home address to DiNes. "How did you—?" she started, but was swiftly cut off by her father.

"Magdalena, please sit. DiNes is here to express his affection for you and to seek my blessing to court you. We discussed this possibility earlier, and now I need to know your decision," Mr. Pondeaux said, his tone stern yet concerned.

"I—I'm somewhat flustered. I didn't anticipate him arriving unannounced; I assumed we would have a private discussion before approaching you," Magdalena stammered, slightly overwhelmed by the unexpected situation.

"So, it seems you had indeed planned to meet him. This implies you've made up your mind about his proposal?" Mr. Pondeaux pressed further, his eyebrows arching in a mix of inquiry and surprise. "Yes, it seems that way," Magdalena admitted, her gaze locked onto DiNes, her eyes reflecting a whirlpool of emotions.

Mr. Pondeaux paused, thinking about the matter before him, his hands rubbing together in contemplation. "I see," he murmured, the gravity of the moment settling around them, ushering them into a realm of serious family discourse.

DiNes could not hold back any longer; he felt compelled to speak, even if it was out of turn. "Magdalena, even though our time together was brief, not a moment has passed where I haven't thought about you. As I have already mentioned to your father, I am fully aware that my reputation is somewhat tarnished. However, I am making genuine efforts to change my ways," he declared, his voice ringing with sincerity.

He paused, taking a deep breath to gather his emotions before continuing, "I want to evolve into a man whom you can admire and be proud to stand beside. I sincerely hope you will consider giving me a chance to prove myself to you." His eyes bore into hers, a plea for understanding and hope shimmering within them.

Mr. Pondeaux, sensing the tension in the room, spoke deliberately, "While I appreciate your candor, DiNes, words are fleeting on the other hand actions endure. If you are genuine in your intentions, you must prove it." With a determined nod, DiNes prepared himself to listen to Mr. Pondeaux's conditions.

"One, cleanse yourself of your past vices; abstain from alcohol, narcotics, or any form of intoxicants and submit yourself to a ninety-day rehabilitation period. Two, your courtship with Magdalena, if she is serious, will take place exclusively here in France, under the watchful eyes of her family members. Three, maintain a respectable image and abstain from any association with women of dubious character or individuals with questionable backgrounds. Four, contribute nobly to society, mark your presence in a manner that beholds respect and admiration."

As Mr. Pondeaux listed out each condition, the weight of each stipulation felt heavy but not insurmountable. Magdalena's eyes never left DiNes. When her father sought her agreement, she hesitated momentarily but then, with a surge of newfound resolve, she agreed "Magdalena, my dear," Mr. Pondeaux began, his voice filled with fatherly affection and concern. "This man harbors intentions to court you, but under strict stipulations. I must know, do his feelings find an echo within you?"

A flurry of emotions danced across Magdalena's face before she finally found her voice, a gentle yet decisive affirmation, "Yes, Papa." The conditions were also Magdalena's responsibility, her crucial role in upholding them was imperative. With a joyous smile that seemed to illuminate the room, Magdalena agreed, her eyes brimming with love and hope as they found DiNes'.

"Well, now that we've addressed that matter, might the two of you be staying for dinner? We have a guest house situated on the west side of the estate; you are both welcome to stay there until morning. But first, let me invite you to join us for tea," Mr. Pondeaux offered, his tone now considerably warmer.

"Thank you for your gracious offer, actually, we are here in France attending to other important business matters. I just didn't want to miss the chance to express my feelings and intentions towards you," DiNes responded earnestly. "We can stay only but one day. I'm afraid at first light, Charles and I must continue on our journey." His voice held a note of regret, wishing they could linger a bit longer in this moment of newfound hope and understanding.

Chapter Twelve

"Parting is Such Sweet Sorrow/Beginnings Are Virulent Joy"

As the morning sun filtered through the ornate windows of the Pondeaux residence, DiNes and Charles made their way to the main house and soon found themselves amidst Mr. Sohan Pondeaux, Magdalena, and her aunt Camila, breakfasting in a room that bore the aroma of freshly baked bread and laughter that rivalled the sparkling chandeliers. With delightful dishes constantly circulating and conversation flowing as smoothly as the fine wine, the grandeur of the Pondeaux household was infused with warmth and hearty laughter.

With an affectionate farewell, DiNes and Charles embarked on their journey back to Marseille. As the familiar landscape of Paul's estate came into view, a contagious sense of joy filled the car. Their previous adventure seemed to blend seamlessly with the prospect of a new beginning, one that was tinged with humor and somber stories.

Paul, always the congenial host, greeted them with his larger-than-life personality, ushering them in with open arms and a beaming smile that could rival the sun. With glasses clinking and mirth filling the room, DiNes recounted their whirlwind adventure, peppered with amusing anecdotes.

"...and there I was, standing before Mr. Pondeaux, pouring my heart out like some lovesick poet,' DiNes chuckled as he narrated, causing Paul to burst into hearty laughter.

DiNes continued with the tale, pausing dramatically before unveiling the final discovery of the gold. When he extended the offer of sharing the gold to Paul, the room dipped into a pregnant pause. They watched Paul as he seemed to sink deep into contemplation, his eyes twinkling with a hint of amusement.

"Well, I must admit, that's quite the proposition," Paul said, breaking the silence with a grin. "But, I figure that I have more than enough to sustain me and my little empire here."

DiNes and Charles exchanged amused glances as Paul paced the room, embarking on an animated monologue about the virtues of hard-earned wealth and the satisfaction it brought him. "You see, my boy, my wealth is a result of sweat, toil, and a dash of charm," he winked, eliciting laughter from his audience. "I think, perhaps, this gold should find a more charitable abode."

DiNes leaned back, a grin stretching across his face. "Well, I have to say, I didn't see that coming. But charity it is!"

Upon his return, DiNes promptly reached out to Dr. Stoge. "I must apologize for missing our scheduled appointment. More pressing matters arose," he began, his voice tinged with a newfound determination. "I heeded your advice, venturing towards fresh horizons. But I find myself in need of your assistance."

Dr. Stoge listened attentively, a mixture of concern and curiosity in his voice as he responded, "Of course, how may I assist you in this new journey?"

DiNes hesitated for a brief moment before continuing, a trace of vulnerability surfacing. "It seems I've been harboring a tempest within me, nurturing a darkness that has consumed much of my spirit. My very soul has become a playground for the devil's desires, and I—" he paused, taking a deep, steadying breath, "I realize I must embark on a journey of cleansing and renewal."

Dr. Stoge remained silent for a few beats, absorbing the gravity of DiNes's words. When he finally spoke, his voice carried a gentle yet firm resolve. "DiNes, your honesty in this moment is both brave and commendable. I sense a genuine desire for transformation within you." He paused, choosing his next words carefully. "Embarking on a path of healing and renewal is a complex yet rewarding endeavor. It will require a deep commitment from you, a willingness to confront and exorcise the demons that have held you captive."

DiNes nodded, though Dr. Stoge couldn't see it. "I understand, and I am ready to take on this challenge. I yearn for a fresh start, a rebirth of sorts."

Dr. Stoge could hear the conviction in DiNes's voice, a spark that held the promise of change. "I am here to support you every step of the way, DiNes. Together, we will navigate this journey, steering you towards a future where peace and fulfillment are within reach."

DiNes's voice trembled slightly as he replied, a wave of emotions washing over him. "Thank you, Dr. Stoge. Your guidance means more to me than you know."

As they concluded their conversation, a palpable sense of hope permeated the space between them, a beacon of light illuminating the path ahead, promising new beginnings and the prospect of true redemption. Dr. Stoge arranged for DiNes to be admitted into a facility located in Abbaye de Lérins. The atmosphere had a more stringent lifestyle as the island had a monastic culture. He felt a facility off of the island would be less tempting for DiNes to withdraw his commitment to sobriety.

DiNes also discovered, through his father's journals, the location where the shipwrecked vessel had been sailed to, and arranged for it to be brought to the cove. Charles and DiNes decided that the dreadful events haunting the ship would cease, rewriting its history so the young Barclay's death would not be in vain. Consequently, the estate thrived, blossoming into a living, breathing entity once more, reverberating with joyful echoes and vibrant life.

Before leaving to the infirmary there remained one final task, DiNes removed the list he had tasked Charles with completing a month prior, looked it over and begin with writing checks to all of his creditors. When he reached the second page he took out his note pad and began to construct three letters. The first letter was to the Mandu's

"Dear Franklin and Mabel,

I hope this letter finds you well. Though it may come as a surprise, it's a sentiment that has weighed heavily on my heart. While this letter isn't an invitation to rekindle past connections, it is written with a hope for closure and healing for all of us.

I deeply regret my past actions and the harm I've caused. My behavior was inexcusable, and I allowed myself to be part of an arrangement that compromised the integrity of us all.

Franklin, Mabel is your cherished partner, and she should never have been subjected to such circumstances. And Mabel, Franklin, despite his misjudgments, acted out of fear of losing you. I hope that you can find it within yourselves to forgive and understand each other, to rebuild the trust and foundation of your relationship.

May the coming years see you both grow stronger together, cherishing and upholding each other in love and respect. As a token of my remorse, I've enclosed what I believe to be the sum of the financial transactions over the past years. I hope you will accept this gesture as a small step toward amends. Wishing you both healing and happiness,

All the Best

DiNes

The second letter was to Amoremea, to her DiNes wrote a heartfelt letter of apology that read:

Dearest Amoremea,

You have been a vision of beauty, pleasure, and desire. I have enjoyed our times together I feel an aching truth: our time together, regardless of its depth, has not nudged us toward a more committed union. For any pain or confusion I may have caused, I sincerely apologize.

I must ask you to forgive me for taking up your time and misusing your treasures for my own selfish purposes. You are a beautiful woman with a magnitude of glory to bestow upon a man.

You are a beacon of grace and charm, deserving of a love that honors and cherishes you each day. My fervent wish is that, in time, you find a partner who sees, as I have, the myriad wonders you hold.

It pains me to write this, but for our own sakes, our interactions must come to an end. Our paths, intertwined for a while, must now diverge. I am releasing you that hopefully you'll find true love. I am enclosing a monetary amount that I feel is sufficient to afford you an opportunity to live as a reputable lady.

Wishing you all the love and happiness this world could ever bestow upon you.

With my deepest Sincerity

DiNes VåsSon

Finally, DiNes began to craft his most challenging letter yet, addressed to Catharine. The vivid memory of the anger, hurt, and torment he witnessed in her eyes weighed heavily on him. It was a visceral reminder of the many lives he had adversely affected during his prolonged period of reckless philandering. In his self-reflection, DiNes recognized that his past actions weren't merely the result of intoxication, but rather a manifestation of deep-rooted egotism and recklessness. With a heavy heart and an earnest desire for redemption, he wrote:

Dear Catharine,

It would be easy for me to merely ask for your forgiveness and hope you'd grant it, but I'm acutely aware that I owe you far more explanation. I regret to admit that during the time of our engagement, I was not in my right mind; my actions, driven by self-indulgence, brought no solace or fairness to those involved, especially not to you. I've tread carelessly through hearts and trusted spaces, giving little thought to the aftermath of my behavior.

Since our last encounter, I've had ample time for reflection. The extent of my past recklessness has become painfully clear, leaving me both ashamed and embarrassed. Though I may not merit your forgiveness, I humbly beg that you find it within yourself to free both of us from the memories of my transgressions.

I promise not to intrude upon your life further. My sincere hope is that you can move forward, free from the weight of our shared past.

With deepest regret,

DiNes VåsSon

During his journey, DiNes came to a profound realization: building one's own happiness at the expense of others, especially when it inflicts pain or misery upon them, is no real happiness at all. After concluding his writing, DiNes secured the checks to the list using a paper clip. He then neatly arranged the bundled checks and the letters in the top drawer of his desk.

Before leaving, DiNes pulled Charles aside to instruct him on the matter of the checks and letters. "Charles," he began, "while I'm away, could you distribute some items for me? Inside the top drawer of the desk in the study, you'll find the list I provided last month, along with checks and corresponding letters."

Charles nodded in understanding, "Of course, Sir. I'll see to it at my earliest opportunity."

True to his commitment, Charles efficiently carried out the deliveries. He successfully handed most of the items directly to the recipients. However, during his visit to Amoremea's, she was notably absent. Without any hesitation, he handed over her letter to a housemaid and quickly left. Charles, driven by curiosity, couldn't resist reading the letter DiNes had penned to Amoremea. He wanted to confirm whether DiNes genuinely intended to sever ties with the woman he often derogatorily referred to as "that Jezebel." Pleased by the contents of the letter, Charles fervently hoped he'd never again encounter her. "Good riddance!" he thought triumphantly.

As DiNes embarked on his intensive rehabilitation journey, the days turned into a whirlwind of grueling confrontations and comical interactions with the stern-faced doctors and monks who managed the facility. These individuals, with a blend of wisdom and rigidity, transformed his path to recovery into a challenge that seemed to have its own life force.

In his letters to Charles, DiNes often found refuge in humor, painting vivid pictures of his day-to-day experiences within the austere walls of the sanatorium. He detailed his futile attempts at charming the stoic staff, who seemed impervious to his charismatic advances. These narratives brought a touch of lightness to the heavy task he had undertaken, giving Charles a glimpse into DiNes's evolving spirit and resilience.

He also inquired frequently if Magdalena had been spotted on the Island, his heart a constant swirl of longing and apprehension. Despite the distance that now lay between them, DiNes could not shake off the deep connection he felt with her, a bond that seemed to defy time and circumstance. He wrote to her a few times but decided it best to keep his distance so that he remained focused on the task at hand. Soon they would be in each other's presence and embark on the life he so often day dreamed about. Magdalena gave him something to look forward too and it made him all the more diligent to overcome his past.

But it was not just Magdalena who occupied his thoughts. DiNes found himself reflecting on the lives of those who had stood by him through thick and thin, especially Maria and Charles. In his letters, he promised them a generous share of his wealth upon his return, a token of his gratitude and a reflection of the newfound generosity that was blossoming within him.

As the days went by, the letters became a beacon of hope and a testament to DiNes's determination to turn over a new leaf. Through his words, Charles could sense the emergence of a man who was no longer defined by his vices, but by his unwavering commitment to rebuild himself from the ground up.

In the quiet moments, amidst the harsh regimen and the stern oversight, DiNes discovered a well of strength he hadn't known existed within him. Every setback became a stepping stone, every failure a lesson in humility and perseverance.

Meanwhile, Charles and Maria transformed the mansion into a bustling hub of activity, orchestrating tours that showcased its grandeur and history, along with organizing outdoor events brimming with laughter and competitive banter. The hidden corridors and secret passages leading to the cove were the greatest thrill.

With the assistance of a few servants, Charles removed the original treasure chest, replacing it with a faux one filled with an assortment of trinkets, souvenirs, and delightful objects. The children who toured the mansion were particularly enchanted, feeling as though they were on a true treasure hunt. As an added attraction, tourists could board the old Barclay vessel where they were greeted by a former ship captain who regaled them with tales of pirates and sea adventures.

Chapter 13 – Closing

"Golden Horizons: A Pause, Not an End"

Just when they believed their adventures had reached quietude, as they were wrapping up, Charles made a startling discovery. While clearing the contents of the treasure chest, he found four withered envelopes nestled beneath the last layer of gold bricks. Hesitating for only a moment, he carefully retrieved them. Each envelope was uniformly aged and slightly brittle, seemingly harboring secrets from years past. Their seals remained untouched, safeguarding the mysteries contained within.

"Maria, come quickly!" Charles called out, an edge of excitement in his voice. Upon her arrival, Charles hastily explained his discovery, holding one of the envelopes up to her, as if seeking her tacit permission to unveil the secrets it guarded. With a nod from Maria, Charles carefully opened the first envelope. Inside, a cold metal key gleamed, wrapped snugly in a piece of paper. Unfolding the paper revealed the letters "SDB" followed by a set of three numbers. The next three envelopes bore the same: keys with similar notes, each having a unique set of three numbers.

The room was filled with palpable tension. The keys clearly pointed to Safe Deposit Boxes, but where? And what did they contain? With a smirk, Charles looked at Maria and said, "Well, it seems our tale isn't over yet. What say you, Maria do you think we three, are up for another adventure?" The glint in Maria's eyes matched Charles enthusiasm. "The horizon is vast, my friend. I'll let DiNes know when he returns. I'll see if he wants to chase it."

"Oh I'm sure he'll accompany you on another adventure, Aye you'll have no problem with his indulgence, I'm sure of it!" Maria chuckled.

The promise of a fresh mystery, interwoven with their shared past, beckoned them forward. As a new chapter dawned on the horizon, ready to be unveiled, anticipation grew. Stay tuned for further adventures as DiNes and Charles dive into thrilling discoveries left to them by the late Mr. Winston VàsSon, Mr. Priviot, and David Barclay. Who else will join the saga? Only time will tell where their next escapade leads...

As for DiNes and Magdalena, is eternal bliss in their future? Or will DiNes's past throw a twist in their plans for holy matrimony? Will Anoremea honor DiNes's desire to part ways forever and exit with grace? Can DiNes truly hold onto his pledge of sobriety? And will Magdalena be able to leave behind the memories of her late husband, Lucas?

Finally will Trudy's holiday gathering be the catalyst in getting Charles and Maria, to confess their hidden passion for one another? Can their love be fully reciprocated, allowing them to settle into a matrimonial haven at the VàsSon mansion?

Though this is a fictional story the **Ile Sainte-Marguerite** is a real Island of Cannes France. Located a mere 15-minute boat ride away from the glamorous beaches of Cannes, the Île Sainte-Marguerite is a haven of tranquility and natural beauty. Spread over 3 kilometers in length and 900 meters at its widest, the island is famed for its fragrant eucalyptus and pine forests which offer a sharp contrast to the bustling mainland.

History is embedded in its soil, with Roman ruins indicating early settlements. However, the island's most famous landmark is the Fort Royal, a 17th-century prison that once held the enigmatic "Man in the Iron Mask." His identity remains one of France's most enduring mysteries to this day.

The island's pathways invite visitors to discover its diverse flora and fauna, while its shores boast pristine beaches with turquoise waters. Birdwatchers find it a paradise, thanks to the numerous species that nest here.

With no cars allowed, the sounds of nature prevail, making it a perfect escape for those looking to retreat from the world, even if just for a few hours. The combination of its natural beauty and intriguing history make Île Sainte-Marguerite a must-visit when in the Côte d'Azur.

Abbaye de Lérins, Île Saint-Honorat, France is where our fictional character DìNes VàsSon spent his time in rehabilitation is also a very real Island of France. It has a vast history of pirate raids and captivating vineyards.

Nestled on the serene Île Saint-Honorat, just a stone's throw from Cannes, lies the ancient Abbaye de Lérins. Founded in the 5th century by Saint Honoratus, the abbey stands as a testament to the rich spiritual heritage of the Côte d'Azur. Throughout its storied history, the monastery has seen invasions, pirate raids, and transformations, but its dedication to monastic life and spiritual pursuit has remained unwavering.

Today, the abbey is inhabited by Cistercian monks who continue the age-old traditions of prayer, meditation, and winemaking. The island's vineyards, cultivated by the monks, produce renowned wines and liqueurs that capture the essence of this sacred isle. Visitors to the Abbaye de Lérins can explore the historic chapels, medieval fortifications, and wander through the aromatic pine and cypress groves, all while soaking in breathtaking views of the Mediterranean. A visit offers a tranquil retreat and a journey back in time, revealing the enduring soul of this monastic sanctuary.

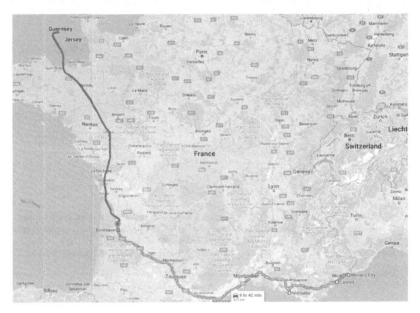

DiNes and Charles's adventure led us on an enchanting tour through some of France's most iconic locales. It commenced in **Cannes**, after a short 15-minute ferry ride from Île Sainte-Marguerite. Cannes, with its famed boulevards and glittering beaches, held tales of film legends and old-world charm, captivating the duo.

From the sun-kissed Riviera of Cannes, they journeyed to the luxurious city-state of **Monaco**. The grandeur of the Prince's Palace and the mesmerizing beauty of the Mediterranean from the Monte Carlo Casino's terraces left an indelible mark on their memories.

Their voyage then took a shift to the historic and bustling port city of **Marseille**. Here, amidst its vibrant markets and ancient architecture, they tasted the essence of the old-world mixed with the energy of modern France.

Further north, they explored **Bordeaux**, the wine capital of the world. Rolling vineyards, historic châteaux, and the aroma of fermenting grapes intertwined with their journey, adding a touch of intoxicating allure.

Their odyssey concluded in **Saint Pierre or St. Peter Port, Guernsey**. Though technically not a part of France, its close ties and shared history made it a fitting end. The charming harbor town, with its cobbled streets and maritime heritage, offered a serene contrast to the bustling cities they had explored.

Throughout their travels, DiNes and Charles unraveled layers of history, culture, and the very soul of each place, creating a tapestry of experiences that would remain with them forever.

Journey to St. Peter Port, Guernsey

Traveling to St. Peter Port, Guernsey offers several options, primarily depending on where one is coming from. Here are the most common ways to reach this charming Channel Island destination:

By Air:
Guernsey Airport (GCI) is the island's primary airport. Regular flights operate between Guernsey and the UK, as well as some other European destinations. Airlines like Aurigny, Blue Islands, and Loganair service the island.

By Sea:
Multiple ferry services run between the UK, France, and Guernsey, docking at St. Peter Port's harbor. The most prominent ferry operators include Condor Ferries and Manche Iles Express. The journey offers breathtaking views of the Channel and the surrounding islands.
Private Yachts and Boats: St. Peter Port's marina welcomes private yachts and boats. It's a popular destination for sailing enthusiasts from the nearby coasts of France and the UK.

By Cruise:
During the summer months, several cruise lines have St. Peter Port as a port of call, offering passengers a day to explore the town and the island.

By Ferry
Condor Ferries is one of the primary operators providing services to St. Peter Port. Their routes typically include connections from:
- **Poole and Portsmouth in England**
- **St Malo in France**
- Other Channel Islands such as **Jersey**

The ferry journey offers scenic views of the English Channel and the islands, making it not just a mode of transportation but also a memorable part of the travel experience.

When planning a trip, it's a good idea to check the ferry schedules in advance, as they can vary based on the season, weather conditions, and operational considerations.

Once on the island, the primary mode of transportation around St. Peter Port and Guernsey as a whole is by car, bicycle, or on foot. There is a bus service that operates routes around the island, making it easy for visitors to explore without a vehicle.

Note: When planning a visit, it's essential to be aware of the travel requirements, such as visa regulations and other entry conditions, especially given that Guernsey has its own set of immigration and border controls separate from the UK.

References

The Ile Sainte Margureite, Cannes, (A Great Day Out on Ile Sainte Margureite Cannes, 2022)
https://wanderingcarol.com/ile-sainte-marguerite-cannes/

Abbaye de Lèrins, (Saint-Honorat Island, 2022)
https://www.cannes-ilesdelerins.com/en/saint-honorat/

Cannes, France, (Cannes A must see city of the French Riviera, 2023)
https://www.cia-france.com/french-adults-courses/cannes

City of Monaco, Monaco, France (DC, 2011)
https://monacodc.org/monacohome.html

Marseille, France, (Sustainable Marseille, a committed and multi-faceted city, 2023)
https://www.marseille-tourisme.com/en/

Grand Hotel Beauvau Marseille Vieux Port (Grand Hotel Beauvau Marseille Vieaux Port - MGallery, 2023)
(Grand Hotel Beauvau Marseille Vieaux Port -MGallery, 2023)

The Palais Du Pharo (The Palais Du Pharo, 2005-2023)
https://www.calanques13.com/en/palais-du-pharo.html

Château d'If (Welcome to Chateau d'If, 2023)
https://www.chateau-if.fr/en

Bordeaux City of France, (Bordeaux, 2023)
https://www.britannica.com/place/Bordeaux

Foire aux Plaisirs: The Bordeaux Fun Fair, (Fore aux Plaisirs: The Bordeaux Fun Fair, 2023)
https://luxeadventuretraveler.com/foire-aux-plaisirs-the-bordeaux-fun-fair/

(Saint Peter Port Guernsey, Channel Islands, 2023)
https://www.britannica.com/place/Saint-Peter-Port

Castle Cornet of Guernsey, (Castle Cornet , 2023)
https://museums.gov.gg/CastleCornet

Made in the USA
Coppell, TX
03 December 2023

25073548R00038